I0783523

Praise for *Under Water*

"*Under Water* is a beautifully crafted reminder that we are not alone, even when we feel like we are."

– Kayla Tellington, Editor-in-Chief of Kaytell Ink

"*Under Water* made me laugh, cry, and appreciate those around me. Diana Elizabeth Clarke did a fantastic job incorporating humor and light into life's darkness."

– Kylie Catena, Author of *Because I Loved You*

"A deeply personal collection of stories, *Under Water* thoughtfully examines themes of loneliness, grief, self-loathing, shame, and inherited wounds. Many times, I found myself with tears in my eyes because of the themes that are relatable and so human."

– Carolina Castillo, Author of *A Song of Magic*

ELIZABETH
PUBLICATIONS

Published by Elizabeth Publications
Baltimore, Maryland
elizabethpublications.com

Under Water is an MFA thesis and graduation requirement of The University of Baltimore's Creative Writing & Publishing Arts program. This book was developed under the supervision of MFA faculty.

The manuscript contains previously published writing:
    "Touch of Roses," KayTell Ink Publishing
        The Encore Issue 3 | 2024
    "The Flight of the Leaf," Washington Writers' Publishing House
        WWPH Writes Issue 45 | 2023

Design, Typeset, and Artwork by Diana Elizabeth Clarke

Printed in the United States of America

ISBN (Paperback): 979-8-218-64749-0

Library of Congress Control Number (Print): 2025906006

UNDER WATER

Stories

Diana Elizabeth Clarke

This book deals with themes of death, eating disorders, and suicide. Please read when you feel safe and are ready to embark on this emotional journey.

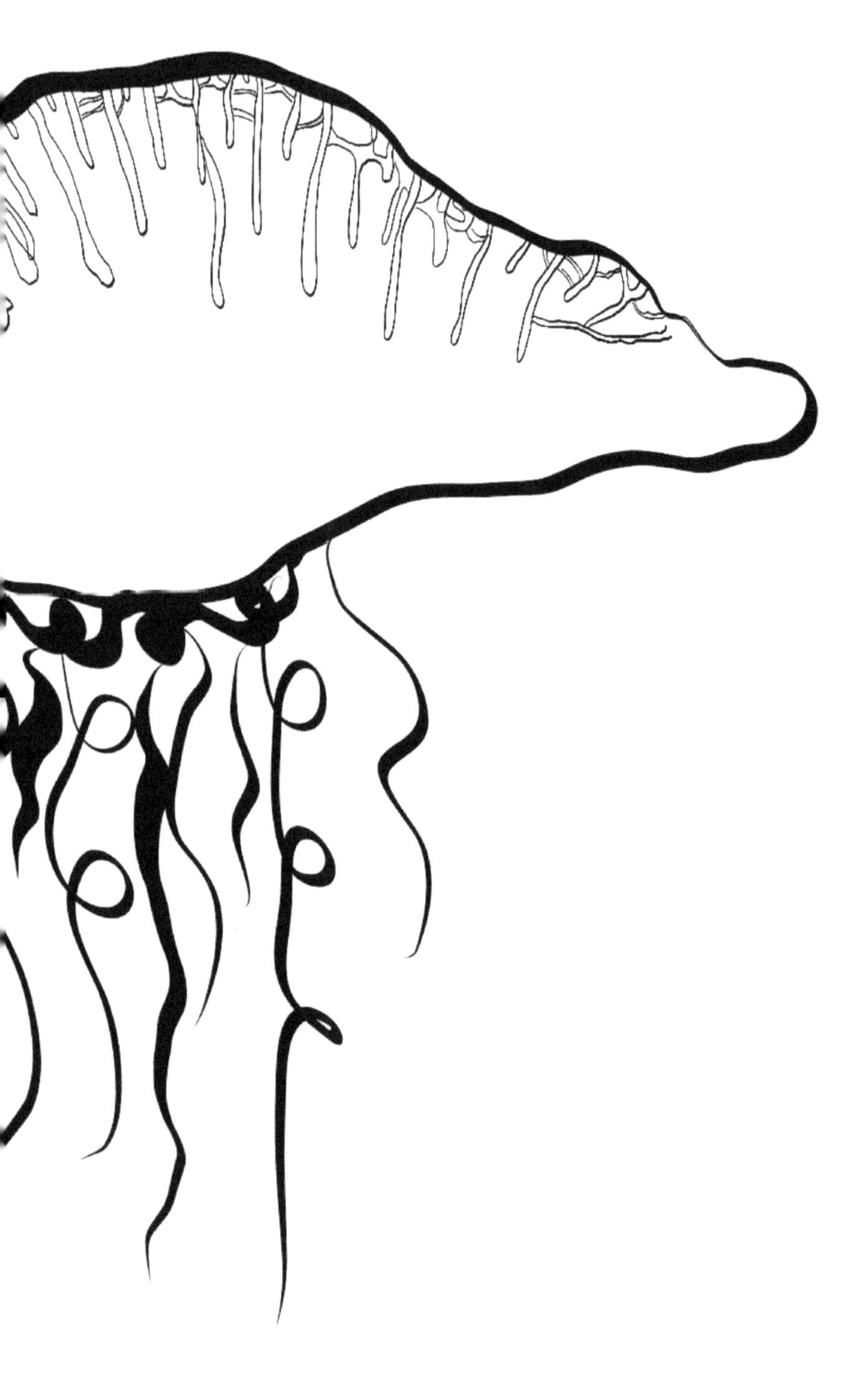

UNDER WATER
Stories

Diana Elizabeth Clarke

ELIZABETH
PUBLICATIONS

BALTIMORE, MD

This book is dedicated to anyone who has ever felt alone.

You are loved.

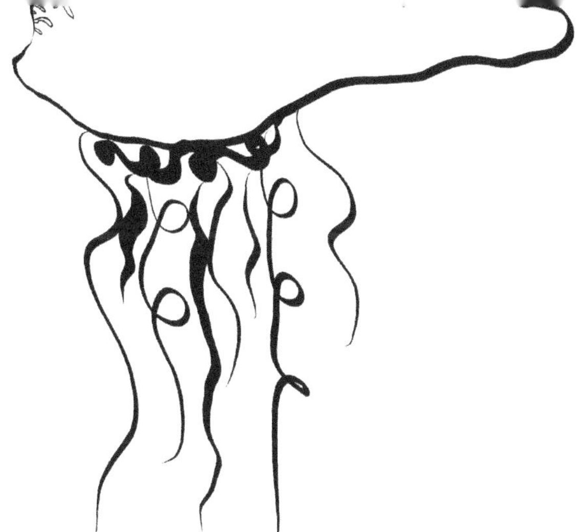

Prologue

Dear Board of Directors,

I understand you wish to defund the bluebottle jellyfish tank. While I recognize the need to protect the aquarium's finances, I urge you to reconsider. I am not writing this letter because my job is at risk; I am informing you that removing the bluebottles from our aquarium would be a great disservice to not only these small creatures but also to our community.

It may sound silly, but bluebottles saved my sister and me. I will not get into the nitty-gritty details about that right now—but I want to emphasize that bluebottles represent a greater good for humanity. We thrive on educating the community about sea creatures worldwide, and that should include the wonders of a bluebottle jellyfish.

To help you understand the significance of a bluebottle, just look at how they function. Bluebottle jellyfish, or the "Pacific Man o War," are clusters of polyps that work together in colonies. Bluebottles join as a family to catch, sting, and kill their prey because they *need* each other to live. A single bluebottle cannot survive by itself. Just think about that . . . a bluebottle will not survive alone.

Bluebottles, in a sense, can be found anywhere—such as a leaf needing a tree branch so as not to wilt. Just imagine, by spreading knowledge of bluebottles we could teach our community a powerful lesson about what it means to support one another. And at the same time, we could protect the bluebottles from suffering. It's natural to be reliant on another for survival, but when you are separated from them or they fail you . . . it may be detrimental. I don't want to fail the bluebottles, so I plead with you to not make me.

If you're still not convinced, let's take a closer look. In the summer, thousands of bluebottles wash ashore on Australian beaches because they are victims to the wind. Simply, they are too small to fight back. Being no more than 6 inches tall, it's easy for them to get washed away. In fact, they don't even swim; they float and can only ride the path the ocean creates for them. While they rely on each other to live— sometimes it's still not enough. That is why the average bluebottle lives for only a few weeks.

Now at the aquarium, our bluebottles' lifespans have doubled— living long and fulfilling lives. Bluebottles will always be dependent on one another, but I work hard to eliminate all the outside factors that just make their lives harder. Bluebottles shouldn't be left to fend for themselves.

Before you make your final decision on this matter, I challenge you to think hard about everything a bluebottle stands for. If you take a closer look at how we as humans connect within our own "colonies," you will find that you have a bluebottle in your own life. Despite devoting my life to jellyfish and working with them every day, I didn't make this connection until I almost lost my sister. And if I had realized this sooner, perhaps I would not have let her feel so alone. So, I plead with you—let us save our bluebottles. We need them just as much as they need us.

Sincerely,

Robin Evana
Marine Biologist, Aquarium of Exotic Oceans

To enhance the reading experience, please enjoy this playlist of songs selected by the author that reflect the emotions of the stories.

Listen on Spotify

Flight of the Leaf
- *Suite Bergamasque, CD 82: I. Prélude* composed by Claude Debussy and performed by Pascal Rogé

Touch of Roses
- *Comptine d'un autre été: L'Aprés-midi* by Plinio Fernandes
- *Interlude* by Alexandra Streliski
- *Roses in a Box* by Elena Kats-Chernin and William Howard
- *Spring 2 – 2022* by Max Richter
- *Opus 18 – Silfur Version* by Dustin O'Halloran

Sunlight in Her Hands
- *Plus tôt (String Quartet Version)* by Alexandra Streliski
- *Gnossienne: No. 1 (Satie Reworks)* by Eric Alfred Leslie Satie and Alexandra Streliski
- *White Flowers Take Their Bath* by Meredi et al.
- *Larmes glascées* by Maxence Cyrin
- *Line Of Sight (Reprise) - Instrumental* by ODESZA
- *Pocketful of Sunshine (Cinematic Version)* by Corvyx

Must See the Bones
- *Vivaldi, The Four Seasons: Spring 1 – 2012* by Max Ritcher
- *Carnival of the Animals, R. 125: The Swan* composed by Camille Saint-Saëns and performed by Yo-Yo Ma
- *Experience* by Ludovico Einaudi
- *Solas* by Jamie Duffy
- *Wind Song* by Ludovico Einaudi
- *The Flying of a Leaf* by Mattia Vlad Morleo

Follow the Water
- *Full Moon (Arr. Lewin for Guitar)* by Ludovico Einaudi, Milos Karadaglic
- *I Skumringstimen* by Vali
- *Nordavindens Klagesang* by Vali
- *Medianoite* by Sangre de Muerdago and Pablo C. Ursusson
- *The Poet* by Bruno Sanfilippo

Cloudless Sky
- *The Untold* by Secession Studios

Under Water Reading Playlist

When Mothers Fly
- *8 Hours, Still No Rain* by Hosini and Jones Meadow
- *Arctic* by Sleeping At Last
- *Autumn Wind* by Yehezkel Raz
- *Turning Page (Instrumental)* by Sleeping At Last

Under Water
- *Breathtaker* by SYML
- *Lung* by Vancouver Sleep Clinic
- *Alcalá* by Jakob Ahlbom
- *Between Light* by Abby Gundersen

She's a Bluebottle
- *Mr. Sandman – Piano and Violin Version* by SYML
- *Fear of Water – Piano Solo* by SYML
- *Elevator Song (feat. Ren Ford)* by Keaton Henson and Ren Ford
- *Not About Angels* by Birdy

*Bluebottles can be found anywhere—such as a leaf
needing a tree branch so as not to wilt.*

Flight of the Leaf

A soft wind rumbled . . . and a leaf lost in the clouds looked for a new home. It was a summer afternoon with green brightness atop trees that danced and sang together with the accompaniment of the whistling breeze. For a leaf lost in the sky, it drifted and wandered above the world. Its new friends were the birds who were once chirping and hopping on the leaf's motherly branches. The leaf soared alongside the wingful creatures—all thanks to the wind.

Morning dew had not yet left the leaf's bright green skin as it twirled, curled, and flew. It crashed through the whipped white cotton of the heavens and shined underneath the burning sunlight. Never before had the leaf been this close to so much warmth. With each wing flap of a nearby bird, the more the leaf twirled in the sky; off it flew into a path the leaf was destined to complete. Down and scraping the clouds to up and touching the daytime star, the leaf glided where the world took it.

The leaf's dew was now gone, completely dried off as the wind sang louder against the nimble leaf. As if an angry man blew a whistle against its stem, the leaf swam down the sky uncontrollably. It swerved between building after building and scraped against brick and metal.

Stronger the wind went and faster did the leaf fly through a city it had never been fortunate enough to see before. This leaf had seen more in the past minute than many trees could see in their lifetime. How was it so lucky?

Wingless . . . the leaf soared like never before. That was until a simple window made of a slick glass stopped it in its path. The harsh wind pushed the leaf against the window of a little old woman's piano studio. Glued to the glass, the leaf faced a quaint room completely empty except for the woman and a black baby grand piano; the piano had no room to breathe against the narrow walls. There the woman sat with her back straight up and strong despite her old age.

Her pianist's hands floated above the keys   drifting in an invisible current—with a limp wrist and fingers itching with anticipation. The leaf stood fiercely against the window glass, as if it was anxiously waiting for the woman to play some music. From the outside, it was impossible to hear any notes, but her hand movements were a music all on their own. The leaf laid witness to her fingers expertly running over the black and white keys with a soft, yet aggressive force. Just how the leaf flew in the sky, the woman's fingers flew across the instrument as if she controlled her own kind of wind; a wind of musical essence and fluttering fingers.

The leaf slowly slipped down the window; the woman began to inch out of view. And all the while, the music stopped. Her fingers quivered—paused over the keys. A frown lingered on the old woman's face as she plopped her hands down into her lap. Clinging to the window now, the leaf got one last look at the woman; tears cascaded down her cheeks as she sat frozen on her piano bench. The wind helped the leaf whisper goodbye before it tumbled down to the city street below.

Bluebottles shouldn't be left to fend for themselves.

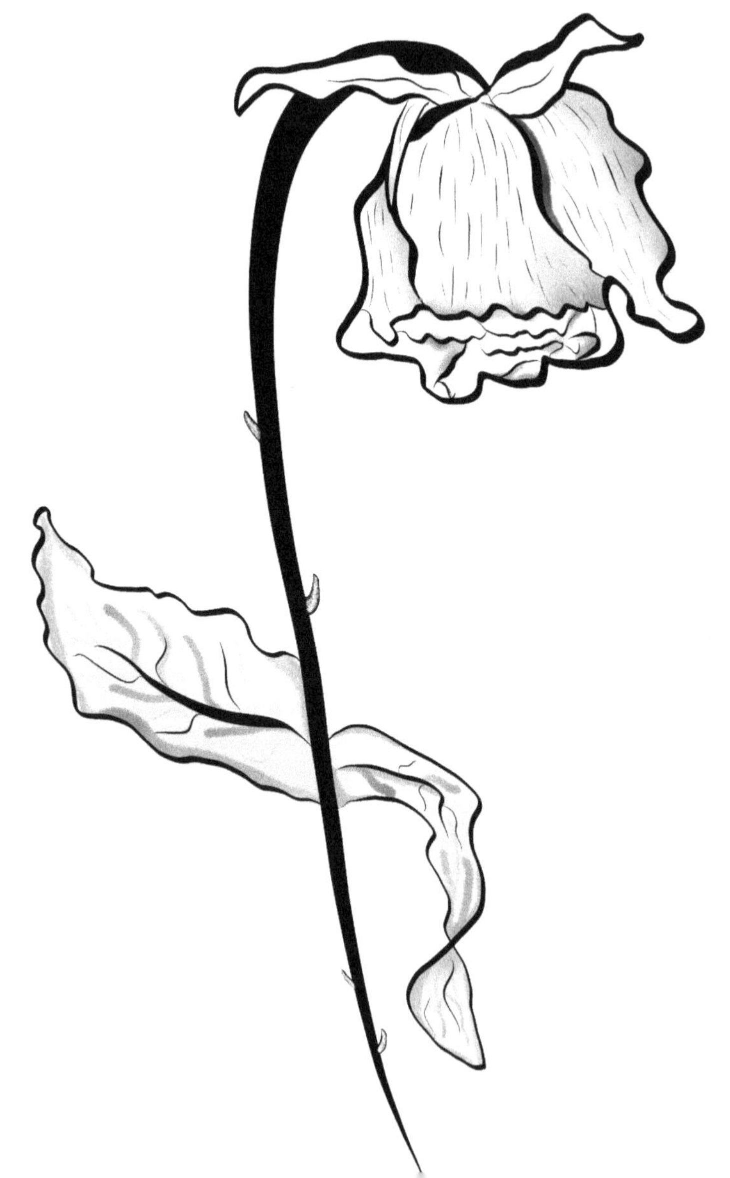

Touch of Roses

Elina walked in the shadows cast by trees as she made her way home. Laughter rang in her ears and her steps stalled when she saw a little girl blowing dandelion seeds into the sky. The seeds twirled briefly until they floated upward and faded into the clouds. Elina couldn't help but smile as she watched. The little girl picked up another dandelion puff, shut her eyes tightly, and blew. Little white flurries floated throughout the air, and the wind brushed one over to tickle Elina's nose. Without another thought, she plucked a nearby dandelion from the ground to join in on the fun.

The dandelion stem instantly turned coarse in her fingers as a once bright green shriveled into blackness. For a moment, Elina had forgotten everything she touched must die—with mournful petals and beauty painted gray. Wilted, dry, and fragile, the lifeless dandelion in her hand was an unfortunate reminder that nature was no longer alive with her simple touch.

The bitterly crisp dandelion crumbled in Elina's hands and her fingers darkened like the wilting flower. She quickened her pace home, angry at herself for forgetting about her magic. Soon, there was nothing left of the dandelion and her fingers would be next if she didn't hurry.

Elina ran up to the boutique she shared with her sister, a small store with a beautifully crafted display of roses in the window. A bell dinged when she walked into the shop, and she sighed in relief as the blackness on her fingers retreated and life was brought back into her skin. Her sister, Delilah, was standing in the corner and her feet were buried by a puddle of rich red rose petals.

"Do you have to be so loud?" Delilah whined. "I can hear you breathing from all the way over here. You're messing up my focus."

"Sorry," Elina said, slightly out of breath from her run. "I had to rush. I touched a flower and needed your magic to stop mine from taking over."

"Then don't use your magic when I'm not around next time." Delilah waved her arms around in circles and more red petals cascaded down from her hands and onto the floor. But within the thousands of petals were four perfect bouquets of roses, ready to be wrapped with ribbon and sold.

Delilah looked over her shoulder at Elina and smirked. Her face said, *You can't do that.*

Elina rolled her eyes as she walked deeper into the store. She began counting all the bundles of roses, making sure they had enough to please their customers for the day.

"Stay away Elina," Delilah spat. "You'll ruin my hard work."

Elina scoffed. "I didn't touch anything. I'm just counting—"

Delilah scowled before she spoke very slowly. "Stay. Away. From. My. Roses." Her hands danced around elegantly again until another bouquet of roses bloomed from thin air.

Elina sank into a corner of the store and just watched her sister be in her own little world. With a little flick, Delilah made roses lightly dust the room. A cloud of roses here, a puff of roses there—it was petals and buds galore. Rose after rose, the boutique's stock for the day was finally created. A loose petal floated down to Elina's feet; she picked it up and briefly felt the velvety texture until it shriveled into a charred lump.

"What did I say?" Delilah marched toward Elina and ripped the dead petal out of her hand. "You know I can't revive what you touch."

Elina rolled her eyes. "It's one petal. It won't be missed." Most days, she felt she was only there to be Delilah's punching bag. What else was she good for?

"What I do isn't easy you know. It's up to me to keep this store running and I need *all* of *my* petals."

"Okay, Miss Perfect." Elina sat down behind the counter and rested her chin in her hands. "I'll leave you to it."

Delilah continued sweeping her arms around, but her feet slipped from all the loose petals on the floor. She barely caught her fall.

"Want me to get rid of those?" Elina asked.

"No," Delilah spat. "I like it this way."

Elina sighed. "Customers can't walk in here. *You* can't even walk in here."

This time, Delilah rolled her eyes. "Fine. Clean it then."

Elina walked around the counter, leaned down, and swept her hand across the floor. The red floor turned black until all the loose petals crisped into nothing. Soon, the floor was sparkly white with no hazards.

Delilah clicked her tongue. "I should make a few more bouquets."

"I think we have plenty—"

"Yesterday we sold out and I can't make more when customers are in here. So, I should make extra today."

Elina shrugged. "Okay." She picked at her fingernails for a bit before she said, "I saw a girl with a dandelion today."

"So?"

"*So*, don't you think we could make more profit if we sold more of a variety."

Delilah dropped her hands.

"Could you make other flowers besides roses?" Elina asked.

Delilah scowled. "No." Her voice was dark, and she avoided eye contact. "And don't ask me that again."

"What? You've never even tried—"

"I'm not you Elina! I can't just touch whatever! I do roses. And *that's it!*"

Elina lifted her hands in surrender. "Okay, geez."

For a moment, Elina thought she saw a tear escape her sister's eyes. But Delilah turned around too quickly for Elina to know for sure. As she watched her sister bloom more roses, her tongue itched with jealousy. She wished she had that; to create life instead of death. Delilah would never understand the burden and the fear she had of touching the wrong thing.

Delilah continued to wave her arms to grow more roses. As her arm movements grew faster, the roses were becoming more thorns than petals. At the bottom of the wall next to Delilah, a thick green vine was growing out of the floor. The vine had sharp, curling thorns and it began to snake up the wall.

"Delilah?"

Delilah didn't respond. She was in a daze of needing to prove herself. But the thorny vine continued to grow, lurking toward Delilah.

"Delilah?"

Delilah continued blooming roses. "They're not perfect enough," she said. "I can do better."

"Delilah!"

Elina pushed her sister to make her stop and touched the vine growing up the wall. The vine slowly shriveled, wilting brown. Elina had to hold onto the vine for a while until it shrunk into black dust. "Delilah," she sighed. "You can't get carried away like that."

"I was fine!"

"No, you weren't! These roses—" Elina picked up a bundle of the new roses that had no buds; they were just stems full of sharp thorns. "They aren't even roses."

Delilah crossed her arms. "That's just because you got me upset. If you weren't here, I would have been fine."

Elina cocked her hip. "If I wasn't here, that vine would have swallowed you whole."

"You don't know that!" Delilah tossed her hair and scoffed. "You just want to make yourself a hero and kill all of my work."

Elina opened her mouth to say something, but she didn't know what to say.

"You're just petty because I have magic that is useful," Delilah said. "And all you are is a glorified trash can."

Tears escaped from Elina's eyes. "You know what, I can't take this anymore. You clearly want me gone, so I'll make it easy for you and leave."

"Fine by me."

Elina ground her teeth for a few seconds. "But if I leave, you won't be able to use your magic either," she said.

"No," Delilah smirked. "That's just you. I don't have that problem."

"Fine." Elina began to head out the door but paused and looked back at her sister. "Just know, I'm not coming back."

"I don't need you," was all Delilah said.

Without missing a beat, Delilah swooshed and swept her hands through the air until a thousand roses fell from the ceiling. A mound of roses sat in the front of the store as Elina exited—her shadow smothered by the magical flowers born of her sister's hands.

Elina's eyes burned as she opened them, but despite her body's pleas for sleep she ripped off the covers and crawled out of bed. It had only been a few days since she left Delilah, but it felt much longer than that. The clock read 6:00 AM and she had an hour before her shift at the local bakery began. The job was perfect for her; she was able to create something rather than destroy it. When she would watch a cake rise from inside an oven, she imagined that's how her sister felt when a flower bloomed.

With heavy limbs, she sulked over to the kitchen window and glanced over the city's horizon. She stared as far into the distance as she could, but all she saw were blurred mountains and blobs of green that were supposedly trees. Past the blurs, on the other side of the peak, was a town she once called home. Elina didn't intend to move so far away, but the only job she could get in such little notice was in the next town. She sighed as she imagined Delilah was in the shop making beautiful roses—

Elina shook away the thoughts of her sister. She didn't need her sister because Delilah didn't need her. "She's happier without me," she said.

Delilah ignored the sweat that trickled down her forehead and had to clench her teeth to stop her fingers from shaking. Her hand was heavy as she lifted it ever-so-slightly in the air—

"Steady," she whispered to herself.

Delilah bit her bottom lip until she tasted blood and forced herself to forget about her sister. She had been up all night trying to get her magic to work right, and all night she had been failing.

It's just some roses, she thought. *Just some stupid little roses.*

An empty crystal vase stood on a small wooden table, and it was all that mattered in that moment. Her arms floated in invisible water, her fingers fluttered, and her wrists danced. Rose petals rained from the ceiling and drowned her feet—but the vase remained empty.

"Ah! Why isn't this working!" Delilah threw her hands up in frustration and rose petals bloomed in the air, but some vanished. Delilah didn't know where they went, and she didn't care. "No, that's not— Ugh!" She picked up the vase and stared at it. "I need full roses to be in you. Not pieces scattered everywhere!"

Delilah slammed the vase back down onto the table. She looked around to see the floor lost in petals. If Elina was there those petals would be gone—

"No. I don't need Elina to clean up my messes." She took a deep breath and stared intensely at the empty vase again. "Not anymore," she whispered before her hands danced again and a bouquet of roses finally appeared in the vase.

Elina's face dropped when the first thing she saw in the bakery was a counter covered with a pile of rose petals. "What is all of this?" Elina squeaked. The last time she saw roses of this quantity . . .

Delilah? she thought.

"Good morning, Elina!" Cynthia, the bakery owner said. She was a fairly old woman with silver-streaked curls always pinned up in a bun. "Look at all these roses!"

"I see them." Elina feared she couldn't hide the nerves in her voice. "Who—who brought them?" Slowly, she pulled her bakery apron out of her bag and slipped it over her head.

Cynthia shrugged. "They just appeared like magic."

"*Magic?*" Elina propped her hip against the counter as she burned the rose petals with her stare.

Elina jolted when Cynthia laughed. "Ain't that silly? Magic?" She brushed a hand through the air as she sighed like a slide whistle. "Doesn't matter where they came from. They are here now, and I have a great idea."

"What's your idea?"

"Rose bread! The counter was cleaned last night so these petals should be fine to eat."

Elina squinted and cocked her head. "Ros—rose bread?"

"Certainly! You've heard of rose water, right? Bread is just water and flour, so what if we baked bread from rose water?"

"I don't think—"

Cynthia continued talking as if Elina didn't speak at all. "Rose water is all the hype. They serve it in all those fancy restaurants and spas."

"I'm aware," Elina said through her teeth. Delilah would always brag that there were so many ways people used her roses and petals. It was what kept them in business.

Everyone loves my roses, Delilah would say, *but no one loves your dead and crinkling ones.*

Cynthia spoke with an enthusiasm that made Elina feel nauseous. "So today, instead of prepping our bread dough like normal, I want you to make rose water first—then prep the dough."

"Cynthia—"

Cynthia waved Elina away. "Don't worry about the rose to water ratio. I went on the fancy internet box thingy when the roses appeared. I wrote it down here." Cynthia reached into her apron's pocket and pulled out a piece of paper. She shoved the paper into Elina's hand before walking back into the kitchen. "I'll start on the cinnamon rolls while you work on the roses!" She called out over her shoulder.

"But—" Elina didn't have a chance to protest as Cynthia hopped away too quickly. Elina just stood alone in the bakery's lobby while a sheet of paper she didn't want dangled in her fingers.

"Chop, chop!" Cynthia shouted. "No dilly-dallying, Elina! You know this!"

Elina gulped as she looked back at the door—her exit. She debated running out now, leaving behind yet another pile of rose petals. "No," she said softly and placed the paper in her apron pocket. "I'm not going to let Delilah ruin this for me." Her whole life, she felt over-shadowed by Delilah, but not this time. She now had a purpose that wasn't just about cleaning up after her sister. With a slight nod of her head, she glared at the rose pile before making a beeline behind the counter to where Cynthia kept a box of gloves.

The clear gloves stuck to each other but slid smoothly onto her hands. They were loose around her fingers and wrists, but it should be enough to protect Cynthia's precious roses from crisping into nothing. Elina scooped a bundle of rose petals in her hands and walked back into the kitchen. Her shoulders were stiff and her elbows were locked straight as she walked—afraid of the petals touching her. As she walked, a few petals slipped through her gloved fingers and left a red trail on the floor. When she reached her workspace, she flipped her hands over and expected the rose petals to gracefully float down onto the metal table. Instead, only a couple fell; the rest were velcroed to her gloves thanks to the static. She shook her hands frantically, but nothing happened.

"What's wrong?" Cynthia asked.

"The roses are stuck to my gloves."

"Oh, those gloves are awful. Just take them off. Wash and sanitize your hands first and it'll be fine."

"But I can't touch them." Elina's voice trailed out as she imagined what would happen if used her magic.

"That's ridiculous! Just wash your hands. It'll be fine."

Elina shook her head.

"*Elina.* Stop asked acting like a child, wash your hands, and touch the damn roses!"

Elina stood frozen, her body stiff with fear. She opened her mouth to beg Cynthia for a different task, but she didn't have a chance to speak a single word.

"I have no tolerance for this behavior," Cynthia said. "Don't argue with me or I'll have no choice but to fire you."

Elina quietly nodded and slowly removed her gloves, careful not to touch any petals. She sulked to the bathroom sink, stalling as much as she could. While scrubbing her hands roughly with soap, she tried to think of a plan but her mind was blank.

"I have to go!" Cynthia called out. "My son's school called, and he threw up in class. Man the fort while I'm gone and don't make me regret trusting you!"

"Okay," Elina said weakly as she exited the bathroom.

She chewed on the inside of her cheek as she looked aimlessly around the bakery. When a mixing bowl caught her eye she thought, *Maybe that could work?*

Knowing she would be fired if she didn't try something, she grabbed the mixing bowl and a cookie sheet. Her plan was simple: use the bowl to sweep the rose petals onto the cookie sheet, carry them from the front counter to the kitchen, and add them to the water. Elina scooped petals with the bowl and dumped them onto the sheet—a few petals at a time. She smiled because it was working, but her face soon fell as her motions created a small wind that caused a petal to drift upward and land on her thumb.

Elina gasped and shook the petal off, but it was too late. The petal was now wilting away. "No, no, no, no, no," she breathed as she watched her thumb turn black.

She looked at the door, knowing she couldn't reach her sister in time. "Maybe I can stop it—"

Elina leaned over the counter and hovered her hand over the rose petals. They had to have come from Delilah—there was no other explanation—and maybe if she was close to what her sister bloomed it would be enough to stop the wilting. But she was wrong. Her hands twitched uncontrollably as blackness grew down from her fingers to her wrist.

She forgot how to breathe and placed her other hand down on the counter to steady herself. But in her panic, she placed her hand on top of other petals. The petals withered away quickly, and not long after so did her hands. It was as if she turned into a wilted flower and someone squeezed her in their fist. What was once her arms was now a dust of blackened roses that was floating to the floor in pieces so small they were nearly invisible.

"*Delilah!*" Elina screamed through tears. "Save me! Please!"

But there was no one to hear her pleas, and soon her entire body crumbled away into nothing. In a deathly silent bakery, all that was left behind was a pile of magical rose petals on a counter—all with crinkled and darkened edges—and a petal trail on the floor that led to no one.

Delilah sighed in relief and smiled at the soft, velvety roses that stood in the crystal vase. *Finally*, she thought. "I don't need Elina."

But her joy was short lived as cracks grew throughout the vase and pieces of crystal flew around the room. Roses exploded from out of the table; dark thorny vines wrapped around the wooden legs and crawled throughout the floor.

"I can fix this." Delilah's voice cracked as deeply as the vase.

Delilah flicked her hands over and over; a prayer burrowed deep in her heart but it wasn't enough. With each movement of her hands, thorns spread throughout the room and rose petals grew five times their size.

"*Where's Elina?*" Delilah cried. Vines wrapped around her ankles and trapped her in a room that was growing drastically smaller. She was pricked and prodded by thorns; her blood mixed with the dark red of the roses.

"I need my sister," were the last words Delilah cried before her touch of roses swallowed her hole, and she was strangled by her magic.

Bluebottles join as a family because they need one another to live.

Sunlight in Her Hands

She woke up for the first time that day when the streetlights were on. Sunset was quickly fleeting and the purple sky was turning black. Stars began to twinkle while the sun was saying good-bye; but for Maria, she was saying *good morning*.

Her head pounded with sleep deprivation despite sleeping for over ten hours; her eyes burned and twitched, painful to open. It was as if she had never slept. Sometimes, Maria believed she never slept and "feeling refreshed" was just a myth. She slowly blinked her eyes open and when she saw that her apartment was dark, she groaned.

"Shit," she whispered. She rubbed her eyes harshly while guilt swam in her gut. Maria didn't want to sleep through the day—but it happened anyway. "Ehh," she sighed in frustration as she slowly peeled herself out of bed.

She didn't bother turning on her lights and instead followed the trail of streetlight blobs from the window blinds' cracks. Maria stopped at her living room window and lifted a blind to peek through. She briefly caught her ugly reflection of tangled dark-brown curls that fought against each other and blue-stained baggy eyes. She pouted because she knew no amount of sleep could cure the dark circles under her eyes. She had tried but always failed. All she could do was be awake when the world was dead. It's what her body wanted, and Maria gave up fighting against it.

She rested her elbow on the windowsill sprinkled with bug carcasses and looked down to the empty street below. Dozens of cars were parked on the street, all with dried water spots on their roofs and hoods. "Guess it rained today," she said with a snarky and bitter tone. "But I wouldn't know."

The world was hauntingly silent; not even the wind or a cricket could be heard. A streetlight flickered and the once bright yellow light dimmed to be dull and weak. She stood there, staring out of her window, for far too long. She didn't want to move—she didn't want to do anything. Maria looked over to her bedroom and thought how nice it would be to curl back into her blanket, bury her head in her pillow, and shut out the world.

"Ugh!" She threw her head back and released a loud and long sigh because she knew that wasn't an option. Although she lived when the world slept, Maria still had a job to do. She groaned as she grabbed her laptop and plopped down on her couch.

The laptop heated her thighs as she worked her soul-sucking job as an email customer service representative. Her job was to read email after email, complaint after complaint, and send corporate-approved messages. Her hands felt heavy over the keyboard as she typed, and her fingers were stiff. The muscles in her hands pinched as if her body was crying, *Please quit your job.*

Maria wished she could do something better with her life—live the way normal people do, see the sun every day, and do a job she would be proud of. None of those were an email customer service representative. But it was the only job she could get where she could cheat out of life. Maria took advantage of the email "scheduled send" button; while she worked at midnight, her boss and customers thought she was working the following morning. No one was the wiser. But Maria didn't want to cheat. She wanted a job where other people were there to tell her stories or wish her a happy birthday. She dreamed of working lunches that were just excuses to gossip and eat on the company's dime. She wished she had someone she could randomly text if she wanted someone to talk to. She needed a reason to leave her apartment.

Maria sat on her couch, responding to useless emails, until her legs went numb. She took the pins and needles in her feet as an excuse to stop working, but when she closed her laptop she thought, *Now what?*

"Guess I could do absolutely nothing," she spat at herself. She did that often because she only had the air to talk to. "Because that's all I'm good for," she said under her breath.

She sulked to the bathroom and sat on the toilet, even though she didn't need to pee. The bathroom made her feel like she was doing something useful, even though it was the bare minimum a human could do. Maria knew it was pathetic, but it was what she had. When Maria noticed she was out of toilet paper, a parade of tears suddenly burst down her cheeks. Her shoulders shook as her arms dangled loosely against the side of the toilet. It was a stupid thing to cry over, but the toilet paper was just a catalyst that let her push out all of her emotions. She needed a long, good cry to make herself feel better. And when the tears were done, she could go back to pretending she was okay.

Maria wiped away her tears and relied on the tiny shreds left behind on the last roll to finish her business. "Did I order—?" she asked as she checked the order history on her phone. "I did," she sighed when she noticed her two-month supply of toilet paper was sitting in her package locker in the apartment mailroom. It was delivered over a week ago, but Maria didn't bother picking it up until it was the last possible moment.

She left her apartment in the clothes she slept in, slippers, and braless. She didn't care that she looked nasty; the trip would be brief and the hallways at this time of night were a ghost town.

In the mailroom, Maria was shocked to see another woman. They were neighbors, living in the same complex, but Maria had never seen her before. But to be fair, she had never seen any of her neighbors. The woman stood over the recycling bin, sorting through her useful mail and useless junk. She looked to be not much older than forty with blinding-bright blonde hair. The lights of the mailroom reflected off the woman's scalp and made her hair shine white. She looked up from her mail and Maria accidentally made eye contact with her.

The woman gave a half smile and a little finger flutter. Maria returned her smile with a face that was half hello but the other half was *I-don't-want-to-be-here-right-now*. She tried to pretend the woman wasn't there to see her in her teddy bear slippers and nipple-revealing night dress as she unlocked her package locker. And if the moment couldn't get more embarrassing, the box she pulled out was coated with cartoon poops; it was obvious she was out of toilet paper and did not bother going to the grocery store.

"Oh no," Maria whispered under her breath.

Now, it was a race. How fast could she grab her poop box and run back upstairs before this random lady noticed? In Maria's hurry, she accidentally bumped into the woman's shoulder. She felt a hot spark radiate in her shoulder and a heat trickled down her arm to sizzle in her fingers.

What was that? Maria thought.

The woman did the weirdest shoulder shimmy. "Oooh," she said as if she took a sip of a strong martini. She turned and looked at Maria closely with an interesting smirk. "I see now." The woman tapped the top of the poop box and looked intently into Maria's eyes. "You'll be okay," she whispered.

Maria squinted her eyes and watched the woman walk away. She stood there, alone in the mailroom, unsure what to think. With her poop box, she made her way back to her apartment uncomfortably aware that her fingers were still tingling.

Maria was unusually tired after the odd encounter in the mailroom. For the first time in a long while, she went to bed at a somewhat normal time and was able to wake up when the sun was up. Her day was welcomed by whistling birds and sunbeams peeking through the blinds. Her room felt warm—rather than its usual chill—and the walls were brighter than how Maria remembered them. She just stared at her white walls; before she was convinced they were gray.

Her head hummed with a sore pain and it was all too easy to close her eyes again. She was about to sink back into her blanket but the sun shot into her bedroom and blinded her. "Ow," she whined as she rolled over, but she couldn't go back to sleep. "Fine," she groaned as she stretched and slowly lifted her body out of bed.

Maria scuffled over to her window and spied through her blinds. She squinted against the harsh sunlight—but once her eyes adjusted she saw the world alive; children were chasing park squirrels, dogs were hunting for the perfect potty spot, mothers were gossiping with babies in strollers, and birds were flying from tree to tree. She let her eyes wander up to the sky, where the sun was burning her window's glass; it was welcoming.

For a moment, Maria thought the sun was smiling at her with an invitation to go outside and soak in the sunshine. She shrugged and thought, *Why not?*

Since she was up before the moon, perhaps today Maria could live the way normal people do. She exited her apartment building and walked across the street to a park bustling with neighbors she had never met. Maria leisurely strolled on the park's sidewalk—the ground heating the soles of her shoes. She imagined herself walking on top of paint bubbles as the pavement was rough and uneven. A nearby tree leaned down to kiss her as its branches were hanging low and the leaves were dangling for their life. She plucked a leaf and massaged it in her fingers—the rich green slimy from morning dew but velvety from the summer heat.

Random conversations were happening around her and one man shouted, "Pick up after your dog asshole!" Nearby, a squirrel played hide-and-seek with a determined dog. As Maria watched life take place in front of her, she took in a deep breath and savored the smell of morning air.

So this is what normal feels like, she thought.

If only she could do this every day, but a sinking feeling inside said it wouldn't last. Today was a fluke, and tomorrow she would sleep the day away. She scratched her head, but her scalp was burning. *What?* Maria looked at the sun in awe because she wasn't standing outside for that long. How was she already sunburnt?

She lowered her hand and her skeleton jumped out of her skin when she saw her fingers glow with a golden light. She held her fingers up to the sky and they turned invisible; they were the same color as the sun. Maria dropped her hand and let it flop dead at her side. Her mouth gaped open, and she stood frozen on the sidewalk. Her hand was glowing . . . *her hand was glowing!*

"What the hell?!" she sang in pure shock.

The longer she was outside, the more her fingers glowed until the golden light crawled over her knuckles and down to her palm. The heat radiating in her hands was warm and oddly familiar—

Standing on the corner of the park in front of Maria was a woman who did a finger flitter wave. Maria didn't recognize her, but the woman somehow knew her. Maria squinted her eyes, but she couldn't place the ginger-brunette hair.

"Have fun with your new gift," the woman said as she approached a car parked on the street.

"Wait—" Maria knew that voice. It was the lady from last night, but she had blonde hair before. It was blonde like . . . her freaky glowing hand. "Wait!" She ran to the woman, trying to wave her down.

"You'll make good use of it," the woman said as she got into her car, "I know it."

"What does that mean?" Maria said, but by the time she got there the woman already started to drive away. She looked frantically between her glowing hand and the street. "What does that *mean!*" she cried to no one.

She stood on the park's curb for a minute or so, but the odd looks from nearby people shamed her into sulking back into her apartment. She tried to hide her hands, but touching her skin was painful; it was like grabbing a pan out of the oven without mitts. All she could do was stare at her hands—scared of them.

At her apartment door, Maria lightly tapped her doorknob thinking it would shock her or burn her or something when she touched it. Nothing happened after testing it five times, so she opened the door and entered her home. Her apartment was brighter than how she remembered it as the sunlight was cascading throughout the walls. Sun pools reflected off her wooden floors and the daylight was so bright that not even the blinds could keep it out. Briefly, Maria forgot all about her freaky glowing hands as she looked around her apartment completely dazed.

This is what I've been sleeping through? she thought.

For the first time in several months, being awake didn't feel depressing. It felt . . . *warm.*

Maria walked into the bathroom and her feet gave out from underneath her when she caught her reflection. Her tailbone now throbbed from the fall, but she ignored it as she peeled herself off the floor and looked in the mirror. She couldn't recognize herself as her hair was now a bright blonde—as if it was sun-kissed. It was just like how the woman's hair was last night.

"I have my neighbor's hair," she whispered while her jaw hit the floor. "I have glowing hands . . . and my neighbor's hair." She ran her back alongside the wall and slowly dropped to the floor, letting the bathroom tile chill her skin. "What is going on!" she yelled as she tossed her hands into the air.

Light exploded out of her hands and sun rays beamed into the bathroom. The room turned into a personal sun haven with speckles glittering around her. The air felt soothing—like being curled up in a big blanket—and her vision was tinted with a soft yellow many would call the color of happiness. If Maria could feel like this all the time, she would never sleep the day away again.

Wait . . .

Could she feel like this every day? Is that what the woman meant by *making good use of it?* Maria stood up and let her eyes dart between her blonde hair and golden hands. "What gift did she give me?"

Sun speckles continued to float around the room; as she stood in a pocket of sunshine, her gut gave her an inkling of an answer. *The sun?*

The sun sparks in the room somehow blinked at her, and her hands glowed brighter and the heat felt warmer.

"What the—? Are my hands? Do they have?" Maria gripped onto her counter to steady herself. Her body felt limp as shock took over. "Do I have . . . sun magic?"

After a long day of freaking out over glowing hands and accidentally giving herself sunburns indoors, Maria went to bed. She was tired and frustrated, having no clue how her newly found magic worked. The moon wished her goodnight as she shut her eyes, and she let the night sing her a sleeping lullaby. She yawned and then snored before her mind was lost in the first deep sleep she had in a long while.

When morning rose, Maria did not. She was still tucked away in bed, ignoring the day and favoring sleep—as she had always done. But this morning was not like the others as a sun-soaked glow illuminated from Maria's fingertips. The longer she slept, the brighter and hotter the glow became.

Sunlight radiated through her blanket and painted the ceiling with watercolors of white, yellow, and orange. Maria's cheeks sizzled and her eyelids were beginning to float open. She released a tiny growl—wanting to sleep some more—but the sun growing in her room wouldn't let her. Her eyes lifted and she saw white cloud-like swirls paint her ceiling. Yellow streaks brightened the sky of her bedroom as sunspots of orange glittered downward to tickle her nose.

The sunspots warmed her head with a pleasant heat and her eyes no longer felt tired. She was alert and ready to start her day. With an enthusiasm she had once lost, she ripped off the blanket and bounced out of bed. Maria lifted her hands and studied the sunglow that exploded out of her fingers. "Did you do this?" she asked her magic.

Although it was silent, she knew the answer was *yes*.

She sighed, mesmerized by the stunning colors that wished her good morning. Through her window, the sun was reaching in to touch her; her indoor magic was blending with the outdoor sunlight. She looked at the sun—which was a bright ball of brilliance—and the guilt that used to poke in her stomach was gone. In that moment she knew she finally wouldn't be wasting her day.

Maria trotted out of the bedroom with energy she never knew she had, but she stalled when she reached the living room. "Wait—"

She squinted at the sun streaks piercing through the window blinds. The streaks turned to rainbows the tighter she squinted, and she just stared at the yellow-orange glowing orb until she saw sunspots dancing over her eyes. "What do I do with my day?"

She grabbed her phone and checked her work email, but there was nothing to do. All emails were scheduled or had already been sent. Maria stood dumbfounded because she could do anything, but she had no idea what she should do.

The sun flashed brighter and caused a sweeping light to brush over the dust and bug carcasses that coated the windowsill. Maria groaned as she noticed the dirt and mess. Her eyes scanned over her apartment and saw all the trash, dust, and crumbs she had ignored before. In the dark, it was easy for mess to hide.

"Should I?" Maria debated grabbing the cleaning supplies she shoved deep under her bathroom sink, but it didn't sound enticing. She had the whole day, free to do whatever she wanted; should she really spend that time doing chores?

She folded her arms but winced when her fingers burnt the insides of her elbows. "Ouch." She looked down and saw her hands glow with a light brighter than a fire.

Maria tossed her hands up in the air. "What?" she challenged the sun.

The sun grew brighter and spread its warmth around the apartment until Maria began to sweat. All the while, somehow every single mess in her apartment was in its own spotlight. It was obvious what the sun was trying to tell her.

"But I don't want to," Maria barked.

Her hands sizzled with a greater heat and the glow of her hands was blinding.

She tossed her head back, defeated. "Fine. I'll clean."

Maria dragged her feet as she began to clean, but it didn't take long for her to get invested. Soon, she was determined to wipe down every inch until her apartment shined. Music was blasting through her phone, and she gave herself mini dance breaks every now and then. Occasionally, she would look out the window and thought she noticed the sun bobbing to the beat of the music.

Eventually, the apartment stunk of chemicals that burned her nose. She lifted all her blinds, opened the windows, and propped open her apartment door. In her pajamas and unbrushed hair, she continued to dance her way through cleaning, completely forgetting that at this time of day anyone could walk by.

With a mop in hand, she tried to do a little spin but froze in horror when she awkwardly made eye contact with the neighbor from the mailroom.

"Hi," the woman said with a smile that was cheerful yet shy.

Maria couldn't help but giggle when she noticed the woman was holding a box covered with cartoon poops. Her neighbor had her own poop box.

The woman laughed alongside Maria for a moment. "Guess we both like to have our toilet paper delivered," she said.

"Haha, yeah."

The woman approached the doorstep of her apartment and briefly looked at the cleaning fiasco before her eyes settled on the sun piercing through the window. "I see the sun is treating you well," she said.

Maria didn't know where the question came from, but she asked, "Did the sun treat you well too?"

The woman nodded. "I was going through a rough time. Divorce, custody battles, and such. It was hard to get out of bed some days." She pointed to the couch and asked, "Can I?"

Maria nodded and sat down on the couch next to the woman. "I'm Maria, by the way."

"Josephine," the woman said.

Maria twiddled with her fingernails. "So, why me?"

Josephine shrugged. "I didn't choose you. The magic did."

Maria darted her eyes back and forth between her neighbor and the sun.

"But I didn't need it anymore," Josephine continued. "It was time for it to move on and help someone else."

"How do you know if—" Maria hung her head low for a few seconds. "How do you know if you're okay?"

Maria jolted when a soft hand patted her shoulder. She looked up and saw Josephine give a gentle smile. "Some days are harder than others. But the sun is always there, even when the magic leaves." Josephine stared out the window and sighed. "You'll never forget how the magic feels. And the memory of it is enough to tell me I'll be okay."

"Thank you," Maria whispered.

"I know you haven't had the magic long, but . . . " Josephine paused to squeeze Maria's hand. "Since that night I first saw you, you look happier now."

"I feel . . . " Maria sighed. "I don't know if happy is the right word, but I'm getting there."

"It takes time. But let the sun help you. That's what it's there for."

Maria looked out her window and watched the sun dance with wispy clouds; radiant beams sliced through puffs of white. "I guess, I did feel happy this morning."

"That's great!" Josephine's enthusiasm made Maria smile because it didn't sound fake.

"I normally don't wake up in the morning. It's nice to see the day."

"I know how that feels. It'll get easier."

Maria didn't know why, but she trusted Josephine and decided to reveal everything. And it felt good to have someone to talk to. "I don't have much to wake up for," Maria said. "My job is awful. Boring, but ten times worse. I want to do something with my life, you know? But I don't know how. Sometimes, I think I shouldn't bother getting up." She felt tears creep out of her eyes as she spoke. "I mean, today I had the whole day and all I did was clean."

"Cleaning is good—"

"But I want to do something more."

"Like what?"

Maria wiped her nose. "I don't want to be stuck in my apartment all day. I don't want to feel alone all the time."

"I know exactly how that feels. On the days when I don't have my kids, I struggle too." Josephine sat up straighter. "I'll tell you what. How about, when you feel lonely you just knock on my door. I live at the end of the hallway." Josephine leaned in and whispered, "I need someone to talk with too."

"Thank you I—I could use a friend."

"Just remember, you have two friends now," Josephine said as she winked at the sun.

As Josephine exited the apartment, a cloud shifted to help the sun shine brighter. A warm glow illuminated the floor and subtle sun sparkles rained throughout the room. Maria breathed in the warmth that surrounded her and felt the sun kiss her. Right then, she had a feeling she would never feel alone again.

She didn't know how much longer she would have this magic, but Maria promised she would never take it for granted. And she planned to knock on Josephine's door soon, perhaps to just say hello.

*The bluebottle's tiny size makes it easy
for them to get washed away.*

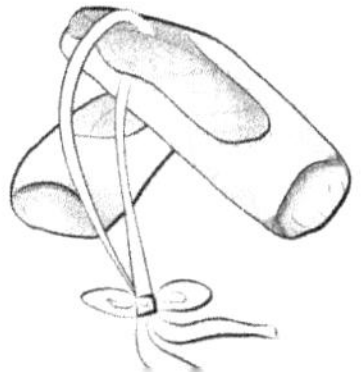

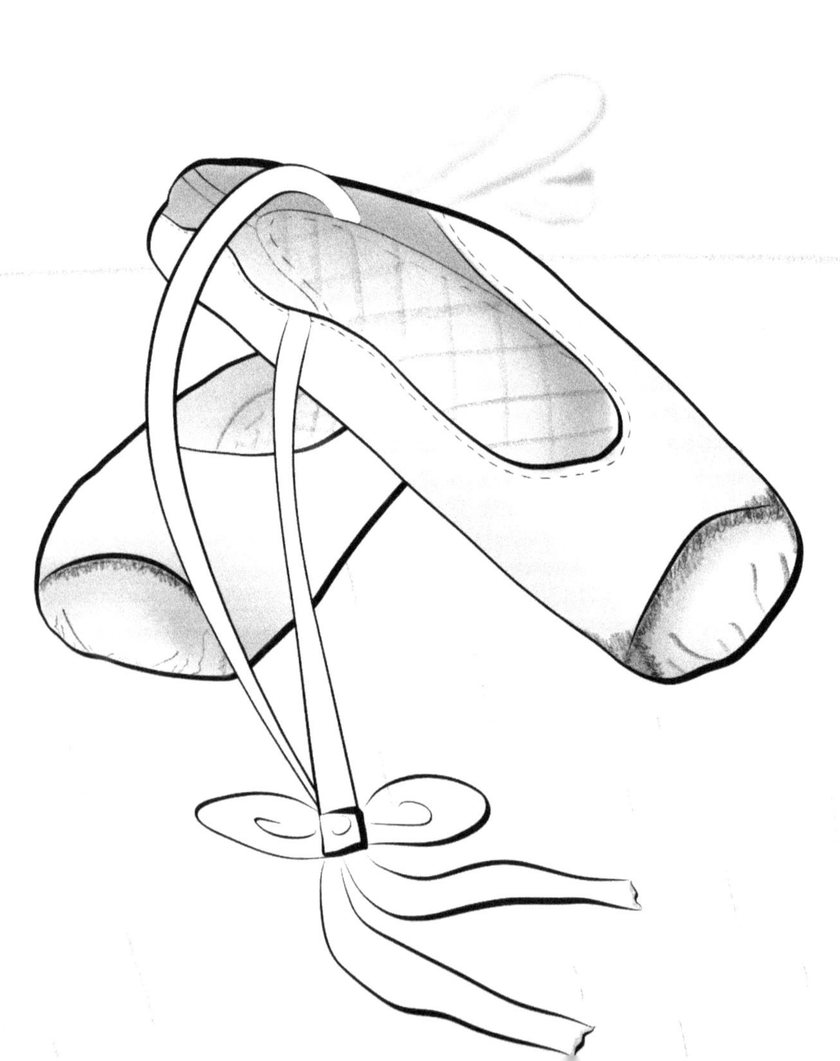

Must See the Bones

I know you have questions, and you want to ask me why. I shouldn't have pushed you away, but I can't change the past. The least I could do is try to tell you how it happened. I danced with death, and I didn't survive my skeletal *pas de deux*. But the day I died is not what it says on my tombstone. It all started last summer . . . June 15th, 1998 to be exact.

You remember the day, don't you? That day was when everything was finally happening for us. We were officially professional ballerinas. It was the only thing I ever wanted because it was all I had to feel Mom's presence. And I promised myself I would have the life she once had with the tutus, pointe shoes, and applause.

I woke up before my alarm rang, wasted no time running over to your half of the room, and bounced on your bed. Wake up, Lillian! I yelled. Wake up!

You groaned, winced your eyes, and slowly rolled over.

Lillian, I whined as I shook your body. Come on! I began to jump up and down, unable to contain my energy. Let's go! Let's go! Let's go!

Annie, chill, you said as you slowly peeled yourself out of bed.

With all my excitement, I unknowingly began to do a horse trot bounce. Aren't you excited for rehearsals? I spoke so fast I forgot to breathe. Today is the day we can call ourselves real dancers because we've finally made it and are working ballerinas and will perform on stage just like Mom did—

You politely but firmly placed your hand over my mouth. Annie, you laughed, slow down.

But we have to get to rehearsals, I said through your hand.

You laughed at me again as you removed your hand from my face. Okay, you said, let's get ready.

My energy intensified as we got into our pink tights and leotards. It was a short walk to the arts conservatory from our new apartment, but we couldn't get there fast enough. I walked too quickly for you to keep up, but you didn't seem to mind as I pulled you behind me with our hands locked together. I couldn't believe I was already living my dream, where most girls my age were still stuck at home figuring out what college they should go to.

We made our way throughout the conservatory, past the symphony hall where there was an eerie sound of instruments sliding in tune. I remember briefly looking back and you gave me a simple grin. I returned your smile, imagining Mom was proud of us as she looked down from heaven.

Eventually, we made it to the ballet corridors where there was a round lobby neatly packed with simple blue couches and velvet chairs. The lobby was cluttered with other dancers prepping before morning company class. Some were sewing ribbons on pointe shoes, some were stretching, and others were doing both. Studying their perfectly slicked buns, I couldn't believe I was in the same room as them . . . let alone be one of them. I had a bun too, but it wasn't perfect; the fly-aways were disastrous compared to everyone else's.

My heart hitched when the dance studio door unlocked from the inside. Out walked Mr. Davern, the man with the money or so they say, and with him was Thomas Balanretta, our boss and director. My guess is they were having a secret meeting before company rehearsals. And knowing what comes next, they were talking about me. I accidentally made eye contact with them when they exited the studio; Balanretta scowled at me, but Davern gave me a wink.

Once the studio doors opened, it didn't take too long for dancers to flood through the doorway and find their preferred spots at the barre. I couldn't shove myself through the mass of bodies as easily as you did; I was the last to walk in. Your bright hair touched with gold was easy to spot as you did some toe curls and ankle rolls at the barre on the far-left wall. The sun from a nearby window perfectly cascaded around you; you had a personal pocket of sunshine at your feet. I nestled myself right beside you—just in a sliver of that sunlight—and began to do the same foot warm-ups.

Annie Jacobsen, someone barked my name from the other side of the studio.

I whipped my head around and found Balanretta glaring at me. My back straightened instantly when I locked eyes with him. I stood stark, stiff, and tall with my feet perfectly placed in fifth position. My fingers were interlocked tightly behind my back and my shoulder blades pinched together; I was the perfect ballerina soldier. Yes? I asked with a voice I wish spoke with more courage.

Follow me, was all he said as he turned quickly on his heels and marched out of the studio.

I briskly followed behind him, only knowing that I had to obey orders. This man held my dream, *my future,* in his hands after all. My throat clenched and my veins were on fire as we slowly made our way to Balanretta's office. After a walk that felt longer than it should have, he gestured for me to sit down in the small chair in front of his desk.

I lowered myself into the plump chair that faced his throne and sat on top of my hands. The silence in the room grew to unbearable levels as he combed through filing cabinets and sorted papers. My nerves took over my body and I bounced in my seat as I waited.

Eventually, he found whichever paper he was looking for and cleared his throat. I'm going to be blunt with you Annie, he said. You're going to stand out too much on stage.

I had no clue what that meant. But I nodded my head and continued to bounce.

Look at that poster, he said while pointing to a picture of his prima ballerina and wife, Julia. She was high on her pointe shoes while her right leg was curved around her in an attitude. Her arms were open and reaching up to the high diagonal as her chest leaned into the audience. That is what I want you to look like, he said.

I sat up as if a board was stapled to my back and scooted to the edge of my seat. I can dance better, I said urgently.

Balanretta shook his head. This has nothing to do with your dancing. If I thought you couldn't dance, you wouldn't even be here.

I opened my mouth to ask another question, but he cut me off.

It's your body, he said bluntly. You don't look like all the other dancers here. See her sternum? He pointed to the poster again before he said, You can see her bones. That's what I want.

I studied the poster again. Her sternum was poking out of her skin and her collarbone was brighter than the stage spotlights. She had a flat stomach, which was essentially invisible in her corseted tutu, and her legs were long and slender. I briefly looked down at my stomach and saw a little pooch through my leotard. My thighs were thick as they spread across the seat cushion, and my breasts . . . Let's just say I wasn't lucky enough to have a flat chest.

My throat was sour with tears, and it took everything in me not to cry right there. I was getting fired before my dream had a chance to start.

You have talent, Annie, he said, and the head of the board is going to bat for you. He shrugged before he continued. If it was up to me, I would send you home. I have critics to worry about, so I need clones on stage with the ideal body. Ballet has standards. But it's not entirely up to me because money talks and the arts are expensive.

Balanretta pushed a sheet of paper across his desk. Mr. Davern and I came to a compromise, he said. We are amending your dancer contract and adding an appearance guarantee clause. With a simple look in his eye, he told me to sign. But as if that wasn't enough, he added, I cannot allow you to dance for me and my company until this is signed.

I pulled the contract closer to me and attempted to read all the little words that were swarming across the white sheet. What exactly does this clause mean? I asked, my nerves burning my throat.

To put it bluntly, he said, this clause requires you to meet the company's weight standards and costume sizes.

I nodded, grabbed a nearby pen with shaking fingers, and did not ask any more questions as I signed my life away.

Thank you, Annie, Balanretta said. You may return to morning class and join the rest of the company.

I nodded again with no words and began to make my way out of his office. I was almost out the door when Balanretta's deep voice made me freeze and slowly turn back around.

If your end of the agreement is not met, I will have no choice but to terminate your place in my company, he said with a tone so harsh it could have cut through bone.

I nodded for the third time and quietly marched out of his office with a determination to never let anyone, *not even him,* take away the one thing I had to be close to Mom.

After that day in Balanretta's office, I couldn't look at myself the same. The mirror was my worst nightmare, but I danced in front of it daily—next to those who were more perfect than me. Including you. During rehearsals, I would stare at your thin legs, twig-like arms, and tiny waist. Why was I the sister cursed with an unballetic body? It wasn't fair.

You had everything. Your life was perfect. Mom died when I was two—I never knew her—but you were eight. You have real memories of her, but mine were just fantasy. You could smell her perfume and feel her warm hugs. I never had the chance; all I had were the moments when I felt an inkling of her spirit. I saw her, you know. While I danced, I felt myself in the clouds and Mom was right there with me. She was glued to my side and would smile at me as I danced for her. And I wasn't about to lose that.

I would dance for hours in front of the studio's mirror, after the rest of the company was dismissed, and practiced late into the night until I was out of breath and dizzy. I set up a camcorder to record myself dancing a *saut de chat* here, a *jeté* there, some more *fouettés*, and never-ending *pliés*. I only stopped dancing when I stumbled down to the floor, my mind buzzed with a thousand bees, the world shook, and my vision blurred. But the night didn't end there.

With my bun loose on my head and frizzy hairs cascading over my face, I watched my reflection. No, I studied it—every part of my part of my body—and picked it apart to list all the flaws. I turned to the side and tried to flatten my stomach with my hands. But from the side profile, I always had a gut. *I'm not working hard enough,* I told myself when my reflection wasn't perfect. And it never was.

When I went home for the night, you were always sleeping peacefully. I didn't bother to turn on any lights and instead stumbled through the dark to not disturb you. I blindly placed the camcorder tape in a VHS and fed it to the TV to watch myself dance over and over. I would watch my thighs jiggle and knew I could lose it all if I didn't fix them.

Every day, it was all the same . . . I would dance until it was impossible to continue, study my body in the mirror, and critique the video from that night. I needed a flat stomach and collarbones that would pop out from across the room. I needed to be the ballet clone that Balanretta wanted.

During rehearsals, I'm sure you saw him pacing around the room to watch us dance. He was a circling vulture who whispered in my ear, Must see the bones. He pinched my stomach to measure the fat and then said, Eat nothing.

I was twice the size I should be, maybe even triple. My job was to blend in and in the grand scheme of things that's the easiest job in the world. Yet, I couldn't do it. I tried. I tried to blend in. I tried to get my body to match yours. Ballerinas are supposed to be clones.

I hid my food when I could—down the toilet, shoved in the sink drain, and sometimes under my bed where it would rot until I could sneak it out for you to not notice my untouched meals. We may have shared an apartment, but we didn't share secrets. Looking back at it now, I wish it wasn't a secret. Maybe then—this letter wouldn't be a letter. But I fell deep and only knew one thing . . . food was the enemy.

I knew I couldn't escape Pancake Sundays, where we would eat breakfast on the floor while we watched our mom's greatest hits on VHS. *Swan Lake, Giselle, Romeo & Juliet, Nutcracker*— we watched them all as she danced the lead role in every single one of them. It was a childhood tradition we never broke.

My teeth softly chewed on small nibbles of pancake while I thought back to the times when we made our living room a stage as children. While Mom danced on the television screen, we would grip each other's hands tightly, spin around in circles until we were dizzy, and giggle as we jumped over and over as if we could fly.

Look! I'm on my toes like mommy, I said.

Yeah, me too, you said as we continued to dance together.

Those were the memories I thought of as I regretfully ate my pancakes. And those were the memories that burned my mind when I snuck to the bathroom to vomit away every bite.

Are you okay? you asked me after the first time I forced myself to gag.

Yeah, I lied. Just a little stomach bug.

Every muscle of mine tightened, all my organs clenched, and I held my hands tightly together to hide my trembling. The one thing greater than my fear of losing ballet was being burned by your look of disappointment. And that's why I became a liar. I made excuses every day, but I went to bed proud I never swallowed a bite.

As time passed, my ballet tights wrinkled around my knees and bunched around my ankles. I found it incredibly annoying how my leotard straps would slip off my shoulders. I couldn't see the signs—what the little inconvenience meant. But you still noticed, no matter how hard I tried to shut you out.

I will never forget the night you confronted me. I was in the dance studio, turning for endless hours like always. Blood soaked the insides of my pointe shoes, but I didn't care. I told myself I couldn't leave until I could see my rib cage.

Must see the bones, I thought. Balanretta's words never left my mind. *Must see the bones. Must see the bones. Must see the bones. Must see the bones.*

I pinched my stomach to measure my fat, just like Balanretta taught me. *Not good enough,* I thought. I clenched my fists and trotted anxiously around the room. *Must see the bones. Must see the bones. Must see the bones. Must see the bones.*

After my chant of Balanretta's orders, I went back to endless *fouettés, jetés,* and more.

So, this is where you are at night, you said. I stumbled out of my turn, out of breath and woozy, and looked over at you. You were in the doorway, arms crossed with your shoulder leaning up against the doorframe.

What? I said, my voice out of breath.

There was a long silence between us before you finally barked, Why are you always at the studio this late?

I'm practicing, I shrugged. I thought I was doing what I was supposed to do. Ballerinas have to practice day in and day out to be the most beautiful on stage. I didn't see a problem with that, and I couldn't see how you didn't understand that.

What for, Annie? Your voice slowly rose louder as you walked deeper into the studio. Why are you hurting yourself to dance?

What? I sang with an *I'm-trying-to-pretend-I'm-not-hiding-anything* voice.

You barely sleep, you're rarely home, and you sneak off in the middle of the night to come back here. Why?

I have to practice, I said.

No, you don't. You stepped closer to me and gripped my shoulders in your hands before you said, You're already an amazing dancer. Why are you pushing yourself so hard?

I stepped back and out of your grip. That's what we have to do, I said. I'm just being a good dancer—

No, you snapped. Nothing is worth *whatever* it is you're doing here. I don't even know what exactly you're doing, but I know it's not okay.

How could you say it's not worth it?! I balled my hands into a fist and stomped my foot. My breath tightened, my forehead creased, and my nose clenched. I'm not doing anything bad for trying to be close to Mom! The more I spoke, the louder my voice became as tears fell out of my eyes; I had no energy to hide my emotions. We have to do *everything* we possibly can to not lose her!

You shook your head and lowered your eyes. She doesn't deserve what you're doing for her, you whispered.

What? I cried. My knees weakened and I felt like falling over, but I miraculously stayed standing. How could you—? I was dumbfounded, absolutely dumbfounded.

You casually crossed your arms before you said, She wasn't a good mom.

No, I gasped. That's not true. You're lying!

She was obsessed with her career, you said. Frankly, like you are now. You *always* say it was unfair that I knew Mom and you never did. But that wasn't true! I didn't know her either. I knew the nanny and the daycare center in New York. I didn't know Mom.

I picked the dirt out of my fingernails as I listened. My head hung low, and I was afraid to make eye contact with you. It hurt to see you upset, but it also hurt to hear my fantasies about Mom were all wrong.

Why didn't you tell me? I asked.

You shrugged. I didn't want to ruin her for you.

I continued to play with my fingernails as I spoke. So, why tell me now?

Because you need to hear it Annie, you said. Actually, I hate ballet.

My heart pivoted down the floor as I slowly raised my eyes. What? was all I could say.

I hate ballet, you said so confidently. It just reminds me of how sucky of a mom we had.

My fingers trembled and my throat quivered. Then why are you here? I asked. Why did you audition with me?

I knew you wouldn't audition alone, you sighed. And when I got offered a contract, I knew you wouldn't sign yours unless I accepted mine.

I gulped when you mentioned the contract. Even now, I wonder if you knew about my weight clause. Did you have one too or was it just me?

I'm not here for Mom, you said. I'm here for you.

That was when I fell to the floor and wailed. You hated ballet and I was so blind to not see it. I was blind to everything . . . all that I was risking. But you sacrificed a lot more than I did, and it was all for me. I don't think I deserved that.

You rushed over to give me a hug and I buried my nose in your hair. I can still smell the apple of your shampoo. I miss your smell, your hugs, you . . . everything. While I sank into your hug, what you said earlier rang in my ears. Was it worth it? Doubts grew in my mind while I leaned into you, but by then it was too late for me to be saved.

Opening night was a few days after that. It was the happiest and worst day of my life, all at the same time. I was finally on stage, getting the reward I worked so hard for. But the glory of dancing in front of an audience was short-lived. The last thing I remember before entering this purgatory of cloud dust and transparent skin is blinding my eyes with spotlights and being a lost swan in stage fog. Everyone saw me as beautiful—I'm sure of it. I was the perfect size; finally tall, lean, and skinny like all the successful ballerinas. Balanretta smiled at me from off-stage, which was a sight I thought I would never see. But it ended all too quickly.

As I danced, my fingers shook while my knees wobbled. I pushed through and ignored it, but then the pain was suddenly gone. The next thing I knew, I was floating above my body. I felt nothing—not even numbness—but heavy and invisible weights still crushed me. The stage curtain fell, and I watched you go through so many emotions while everyone else stood helplessly around you.

I screamed alongside you, desperate to be heard. I'm here, I cried. Let me go back, I begged in hopes someone was listening. Let me go back! I continued to scream until the theatre was dark and empty—everyone gone to live on without me.

I'm sorry Lillian. I'm sorry I left you like Mom did all those years ago. Do you feel just as alone as I do right now? Oh, I hate what I've done. I hate what I did to you. I would give anything to spend one more day with you. I never got a goodbye because I didn't know—

So, I'm writing to say goodbye now. You don't need me haunting you, peeking over your shoulder for the rest of your life. As much as I don't want to say it, you'll be okay without me Lillian. You were always stronger than me, in many ways. But if this letter somehow gets to you, promise me one thing. Promise me you will go after your own dream, and not mine. You deserve that.

And I'll be here, waiting. I don't know when or how I will see you—but someday we will be together again. Until then . . . I'm sorry I left you.

Love,

Annie

Bluebottles need us just as much as we need them.

Follow the Water

Mother's coughing kept me awake all night, but I didn't wish she was quiet. Silence would mean she was gone. The doctors said Mortias was incurable, and it was a gamble if you could survive it. I had a cough too, but mine went away in a few days when Mother only got worse.

Morning sunlight shined through the gaps in our log house roof, and the house was eerily quiet. I jumped out of bed and forgot how to breathe until I heard Mother wheeze. She was still alive. I exited the room and headed to Mother's bed, which would be in the kitchen if it wasn't for the thin curtain. Ever since I was little, Mother insisted I have the only bedroom in the house, and she took the bed that was barely a bed; she said I would dream better in a real room.

I pulled back the curtain and watched her sleep in bed. My heart ached as I studied how slowly she breathed; I could see her pain and feel her struggle. For a few seconds, I thought she stopped breathing—but the bitter silence was eventually broken with a big gasp as Mother caught her breath again. It took everything in me not to cry right then and there.

I gently pushed her shoulder to wake her. "Mother?"

She fluttered her eyes open. "Hannah?"

"How are you feeling?"

She swallowed and I could tell it was painful. She didn't answer my question, but she didn't need to. I knew she wasn't doing okay.

"Are you hungry?" I asked her.

Mother nodded slowly and I went to the kitchen. I wasn't the best cook, and you could say I was the worst. My sweet bread was baked sour, and my oatmeal was always burnt. Mother ate whatever I made without complaint, but I struggled to swallow a bite. I followed Mother's recipes and did everything she told me, but I still couldn't do it right. It was one of the many things I struggled with.

I sat in a lopsided chair while I watched Mother slurp her breakfast. I had to rebuild the chair when it broke after Mother fell during one of her coughing attacks. Nails were sticking out of the legs, and you had to balance in the seat to not fall over. I knew it tore Mother up inside that she couldn't fix it herself.

She took pride in doing everything and loved that I didn't have to lift a finger. "I've made many mistakes in my life," she would say, "but the one good thing I've done is care for you."

I grabbed Mother's bowl when she was done eating and went to go wash it, but she stopped me. "Hannah," she said with a weak and raspy voice. Mother grabbed my hand and clutched it to her chest. "I feel myself growing weaker." She coughed a few times before she continued. "I need to know you'll be okay when I'm gone."

"No, no," I said with teary eyes. "You won't go. I won't let you."

"I don't think we have a choice, Hannah."

I shook my head while tears crawled their way up my throat. My breath quickened and my eyes blurred with fear and panic. "There has to be a way to stop this," I cried.

"Hannah—"

Just then, I remembered the gossip I heard in town the other day. The witch healer, Sancia, was supposed to be in the market this week. Healers were traveling witches known to grant miracles for a price—and I needed a miracle now.

"I can ask a healer for help," I said enthusiastically.

Mother shook her head, her hair matting against the pillow. "No. Don't beg a witch."

"Magic can save your life," I said while I squeezed her hand.

Mother squeezed my hand back, and she trembled as she did so. "They'll only trick you. You can't trust magic."

"If it means you won't die, I'll let any witch trick me. I don't care about the money."

"Hannah—"

I let go of her hand and marched over to the front door to grab my boots.

"Hannah. Don't leave me."

I ignored Mother's pleas. I truly believed Mother was wrong, and magic was the answer. "I'll be back," I said right before I left. "I'll save you, you'll see."

The market was unusually quiet this morning with only a few stragglers strolling down the dirt path. I kicked up some dirt as I ran, urgently looking for the witch healer. I had never been to a witch before, so I didn't know what I was looking for but knew it would be magical when I found it.

It didn't take long for me to get to the end of the market road, where a large deep sea blue tent stood before me that sparkled in the sun. That must be it, because what else could it be? A line of twenty or so people stood in front of the tent, but just as quickly as they went in—they left.

Wow, I thought. *Healer Sancia must be the fastest witch alive.*

As I got closer and slid myself in line, I noticed the distraught faces of the townsfolk who exited the tent. I watched closely: they entered hopeful and exited depressed. I gulped and breathed heavily as I waited in the line full of anxious people like me. I let my eyes drift upward and studied the sun high in a bright blue sky, but the clouds looked sad. Whisps of gray spread through the sky and the further out I looked, the darker the clouds became.

Time slowed as I waited for my turn to enter the tent, and all I could hear was Mother's coarse breath and endless coughs. It was a haunting melody that never left my mind. *Please save her,* I pleaded quietly.

"Who's next?" a whimsical voice called from inside the tent.

It was my turn.

"Healer Sancia?" I spoke out softly as I entered. Inside the tent, it was complete darkness with nothing to look at except for what was in your imagination.

"Come in child," an old woman sang. "I've been waiting for you."

Light from a dozen or so lanterns suddenly illuminated the tent and the walls sparkled with some sort of magical gold dust. The tent was surprisingly empty except for a large woven rug on the ground and a wrinkling woman who sat on top of it.

"You knew I was coming?" I said as I walked deeper into the tent. I shouldn't have been surprised because magic was, well, magic. My heartbeat quickened as I sat down on the rug in front of the woman who held Mother's life in her hands.

The woman's lips were pursed and her eyes were what I could only describe as "mean." Until . . . they weren't. She abruptly exploded in laughter, her eyes lost behind her smile line wrinkles. "No," she said bluntly. "But I scared ya, didn't I?"

"Oh," I forced out a little chuckle. I had never met a witch healer before, but this woman in front of me was not what I was expecting.

"I'm Healer Sancia and welcome to my healing tent. What's your name dear?"

"Hannah," I stuttered.

"So, Hannah, what do you want?" Sancia said as she interlocked her fingers together and circled her thumbs over and over. Her face had a thin lip smile like a drunk dog.

My body turned to ice as thousands of words flooded my brain. What should I say to convince her to save Mother? I had one chance, and I couldn't ruin it.

"Come on girl, I don't got all day," Sancia said with an eye roll.

I cleared my throat. "My mother . . . "

"You have a mother," she said. "Congratulations."

"No, uh." I let myself sink into the lumpy ground and the rug scratched my legs, but it was a nice distraction until I figured out what exactly I wanted to say. "My mother is sick," I said softly. "It—it's deadly. Mortias."

The air thickened and Sancia's face fell. For a moment, she stopped being a person and instead was carved out of stone.

"I'm sorry," was all she said.

I leaned in closer. "You're my only hope—"

She held up a hand and I paused. "I can't give you a cure," she whispered.

"But you're a Healer? You have magic!" My mouth hung open as if my lips had forgotten how to move.

"Not that kind of magic," she said in a sing-song voice that only made my insides boil.

This had to be a joke, that was the only explanation. My only saving grace, and Mother's . . . there had to be an answer. "No," I said sternly. "I don't believe that. You're a Healer. You travel the world to help people who need a miracle. Please! I'm begging you to save my mother."

Sancia and I listened to a concert of crickets while neither of us moved. Eventually, Sancia broke the silence when she said, "There's no cure."

"Try again," I scowled.

"No cure."

"Nope. Try again."

Sancia squinted her eyes.

"You're a Healer." At that moment, I didn't recognize my voice as I spoke to a woman who was a stranger less than two minutes ago. Where this confidence came from, I don't know, but I knew I wasn't backing down. "I'm not leaving until you heal my mother."

Sancia sighed. "I know what it's like," she said, her eyes dark with a sadness I had never seen before. "I know what it feels like to watch someone you love die. It's terrible knowing there's nothing you can do to stop it, but you can spend time with them during their last moments. Heed my advice." As Sanica spoke, she ground her teeth. "Leave this tent and say your goodbyes while you can."

"No," I squeaked. The depressed faces of everyone exiting the tent now made sense, but I still refused to believe it. "I won't accept that answer."

Sancia scoffed. "There's nothing else I can give you."

"Liar!"

Sancia furrowed her brows, and her pupils shined with a fire of anger. "I may be a liar, but I'm not lying about this. I'm sorry dear, but your mother is dying. Say your goodbyes because you'll regret it if you don't."

"I'm not leaving until you help her," I said through my teeth. Just like Sancia, my eyes were filled with anger.

"You're wasting your time with me girl, when you should be spending time with your mother."

"I'm here to save my mother." My voice cracked with tears and my entire body felt as though I had a fever—a warmth from terror and a chill from heartbreak. My blood boiled with frustration as I scowled. I went against Mother's wishes to be here, and Sancia wasn't willing to do anything.

Sancia released an annoyed sigh as if she had given up. "You want magic. Fine! I'll give you magic." Sanica rocked forward and positioned herself on top of her knees. She leaned in so close that her nose was about to touch mine. "I grant silly wishes for those who choose to believe in it. This—" she waved her hands around the tent. "This is a show. That 'magic dust' on the wall are teenie-tiny mirrors I glued on to reflect the lantern lights that I control with a battery remote hidden in my pocket."

I turned my head to study the dusted walls and noticed the glitter was the same color as the warmth of the lantern flames. My back slouched and the small tent now felt even smaller.

"The so-called miracles you think Healers do is just psychological trickery," she continued. "If you came asking to be young forever, I would have given you a bottle of my pee and said it was an anti-aging potion." She cocked her head slightly to the side and burned me with her glare. "Is that what you want?! A bottle of my pee?"

It was a sham. All of it: this tent, the magic, the hope . . . all of it was a lie. "Is magic even real?" I cried, still praying that it was.

Sanica shrugged and made a sound that sounded like a mumble of *I-don't-know.* "Could be. I just don't have any."

I massaged my temples as my jaw fell off my face. I couldn't believe this. Mother couldn't be right, because that would mean—

I forgot how to breathe as I thought about how many more days Mother had left. Two? Five? Maybe one? And I was helpless to stop it. "Why not just give me a show?" I whined.

"Because I didn't want to give you false hope." Sancia said softly. "I wanted to give you a chance to say goodbye. Take advantage of the time you have left."

"I can't say goodbye," I cried. "That's why I'm here. I'm desperate!"

Sancia cocked her head, and her voice lowered. "How desperate?"

"I'd do anything."

"What does your mother mean to you?" Sancia barked.

"What?"

"What does she mean to you!" Sancia slammed her palms into the ground and plopped her bottom back onto the rug. "Twenty-five lost souls came to me today wanting magic to cure an incurable disease.

And all twenty-five of them walked out of this tent to say their good-byes. But you . . . " She got onto her feet, walked right up to me until my knee was touching her ankle, and stared me down. "But you are different. I want to know why."

"I—I love my mother?"

"Try again." Sancia used my words from before against me. I don't know why this question was so difficult to answer. Mother was dying and a daughter's duty was to save her. That's how the world worked.

"It's been only Mother and I my whole life," I said. "I don't have a father."

"And?"

"And what?" My voice quivered and my throat was already soar from tears. "My mother is dying and I want to save her."

"Because?"

"Because I—because . . . " My voice trailed off until I spat out, "I can't live alone!" I covered my mouth, embarrassed that I had actually said it.

Sancia's face spread in a wicked smile. "Go on."

I slowly removed my hands from my face and bit my lip to stop my tears. "I don't know how to take care of myself." Once the words started coming out, I couldn't stop them. "Mother did everything. She fixed the house, made my clothes . . . I can't live alone. I wouldn't know what to do." I brought my knees up to my chest and I buried my face in them. "If she's gone, it's just me to rot away alone in a house that's already falling apart."

Sanica snapped her fingers and spread her mouth in an overly large smile. "There it is!" She walked over to a back corner of the tent. "I may have something."

I lifted my head hesitantly. "A bottle of pee?"

"No." She grabbed a dusty book and turned back around. "Unless you want some?"

I wasted no time shaking my head. "I don't want a bottle of pee."

"Fair enough, but I do have some pretty good pee." Sancia sat down next to me and blew a large smoke of dust off the book. "The old woman who recruited me into this life of 'magic' gave me this book. She was the biggest con woman I know, a true inspiration."

"Ok—?"

"Don't interrupt," Sanica scolded. "I'm trying to help you."

I urgently nodded my head in silence.

Sancia flipped through her book that looked to be centuries old, with browning pages and torn edges. "There's this riddle, rumored to be written by the Sun Gods." She slouched and looked up into the air. "Or was it the Gods of Night?" She waved her thought away with her hand. "Either way, it's a long shot. I don't know if it's real or not, but there's a slight chance it is." She chuckled like a hyena. "You're desperate, right?"

I nodded again.

"Well, brace yourself. With the magic in this riddle, you'll be able to trade your life with your mother's."

"What does that mean?"

"What do you mean *what does that mean?*" She was mocking me. "You die. She lives."

I swallowed and my air tasted bitter. Sancia looked me straight in the eye, but her glare sliced right through me like I was already a ghost. I came for a miracle, but I never would have imagined that miracle would be a sacrifice some would consider suicide.

"What's the riddle?" I asked.

She read the riddle slowly and mysteriously, but something told me she just wanted to be dramatic.

Follow the water to the swatch of sea ruffled by winds.
Enter a garden of delicate coral sheltered by storms.
Endure to a magical and fragile place where there's no sunset on the forest floor.
There, you can have what you've always wanted, but with trade only.
Break forth into light, and journey with your heart no more.

"So . . . ?" I leaned over to reread the riddle from Sancia's book. I shocked myself by considering this, but if there was a chance to save Mother—I had to take it, right?

The air stood still, the world slowed down, and time paused for me as my mind rambled. Mother took care of me my whole life, praised me for just simply existing, and I never felt deserving of the glory she showered me with. Even when she was sick and dying, she gave me the bedroom as she claimed the rickety bed that had more straw than mattress. This was my chance to make it up to her, to gift her with the life she had sacrificed when I was born. She could explore the world and adventure, things she always wanted to do but never could since I dragged her down.

"When you're older, promise me you'll leave this place," Mother said to me once.

"Why would I leave you?" I was young at the time, barely twelve, and couldn't believe Mother wanted me gone.

"Promise me."

"Why?"

"Find adventures. Leave no sight unseen." She curled a piece of my hair behind my ear. "Do the things I never got to do."

Endure to a magical and fragile place, the riddle said. Maybe I could keep my promise—go out in the world and see things—but also give Mother the chance to find her own adventure without me. Now was my chance to give her life back to her; she would make no more sacrifices . . . but only after I make the biggest sacrifice of all.

"Basically, you follow the steps to find a magical place to then trade your life?" I asked.

"Yup." Sanica snapped the book closed and the sound echoed. "Follow the riddle, save the life you want, and then you explode."

"*I will explode?*"

Sancia shrugged. "Break forth into light is what it says, but I like to think that means you explode." She blinked at me a few times, her drunk dog smile returning. "So, Hannah? Will you follow the water and give up your life for your mother's?"

Mother had made a lot of sacrifices for me over the years, and I mean a lot. She worked two factory jobs so I wouldn't have to sell flowers on the street. Mother broke her back to give me an easy life. How could I undo all her hard work of taking care of me? I was her legacy . . . the only thing she had contributed to this world. Was it fair to force her to live alone, just because I wasn't brave enough to be alone? My brain was scrambling back and forth, between go and don't go; save her or let her die.

"I . . . do I have to decide now?" I asked quietly.

Sancia lowered her eyelids and tilted her head. "Didn't you say she was dying?"

"Yes, but—" I buried my face in my hands and whined, "I don't know what to do!"

"Stop it. You look ugly when you cry."

I peeked through my fingers and squinted at her with a pout.

Sancia groaned as she rolled her eyes. "Take your time thinking about it, you indecisive child. If you decide to follow the water, come find me and I'll help you get started on your journey."

I sniffed as I nodded. "Thank you."

Sancia waved me away. "Now shoo. You have some goodbyes to get to, don't you?"

It wasn't until looking back at this moment that I realized Sancia got what she always wanted: for me to do what I was dreading and say goodbye to Mother. If I chose to follow the water, I would have to accept that I would never see Mother again. And if I didn't follow the water, Mother would slip away right before my eyes. Either way—no matter what I chose—I would have to say goodbye.

I peeled myself off the rug and sauntered out of the tent. Just like the twenty-five who came before me, I went into the tent hopeful and exited depressed. I looked at the people in line and watched their faces drop as they saw the turmoil in my eyes. But they would never know the cause of my dread as I was faced with the largest decision of my life and Mother's.

I felt droplets of rain hit the top of my head as I sauntered home. I looked up and was shocked to see the bright sun from earlier was gone. All I saw in the sky were dark clouds looming over me. My feet sank in mud puddles from the dirt, but I walked as slowly as possible; I didn't care that I was drowning in a cold rain. I needed more time. But I wish I knew then that I didn't have time.

My steps were heavy, and I ignored the mumbled chitter-chatter going through the market. I let my eyes wander and looked for a sign from the Gods, the universe, something, or anything to give me an answer. Was it selfish to not save her, or was it selfish to save her? Am I allowed to be selfish here, or am I supposed to be selfless? Every answer I came up with seemed to contradict itself.

I stopped walking, not sure which steps I should take next. By the time I got home, I should know which goodbye to make; either I would leave or would watch Mother die. Since I didn't have an answer, I just stared at the fork in the road. To my right was the dirt path that would lead to our log house. But on the left was a path I never thought to take before.

The rain fell harder and created a river in the dirt road. The ground was slanted downhill slightly and caused a current of water to rush down the pathway on the left. Was that it—the water I was supposed to follow? Mud spread up my ankles, like a disease wanting to suck away my life, and I stared at the water. The path looked to be never-ending and there was no way to tell if this river created by rain would take me to a "sea ruffled by winds"— whatever that meant.

I started to step forward—but my toe hovered in the air. I didn't know if Mother was ready to leave this life, but as the rain tapped against the ground, I knew I wasn't ready. Not yet anyway.

A harsh breeze brushed against my face and a wind whistled in my ear. It sounded just like Mother's coarse breath. A tear slid down my cheek and my lips quivered as the image of Mother on her death-bed haunted me. No matter what decision I made, I would be a terrible daughter if I didn't let Mother choose. It was her life just as much as mine. I had a suspicion of what her answer would be; she would want me to live. But I couldn't decide without her.

I walked away from the rain river and quickened my pace to get home. I braced myself for what she would say, but whatever the outcome—I would feel better that it came from Mother and not me.

"Mother?" I said as I walked through the door. "I'm home."

There was no answer—no coughing, no wheezing, and no breathing. I waited and watched impatiently for the catch of her breath, but it never came.

"Mother?" I whimpered. My throat could barely speak behind my tears. "Mother?"

I shook her shoulders, but there was no response. "Mother!" I cried endlessly while I shook her harder and harder. With each shake, her head flopped from side to side . . . lifeless.

The rain echoed my screams as I fell to the floor, not caring that I hit my knee on the frame of her bed. My kneecap throbbed, but that pain was nothing compared to the heartbreak that shattered my body. The air in the house was crushing and my ears ached from listening to my cries. Despite being inside, I still felt the rain hit the top of my head thanks to the gaps in the roof. The sky was crying with me.

Following the water was no longer a question; the universe had decided for me, and I missed my one chance to say goodbye. To this day, my biggest regret was wasting time looking for a miracle that may or may not have existed. I should have listened to Mother. I should have accepted what she was telling me. *Don't leave me,* were the last words she said to me.

"Why didn't I listen?" I wailed.

There was no way of knowing when Mother would draw her last breath, but I could have made sure I was there for her. I wish I was there to spend Mother's last moments with her. But I was selfish; my fear of living alone caused Mother to die alone. I will never forgive myself for that. Being together—even in the toughest of times—is always better than battling things by yourself.

Cloudless Sky

My pain is real. My pain is not imaginary, she thinks. Nova stares up at a blank sky while standing on the roof patio of her downtown apartment. The city looks lonely from six stories high; yet somehow, it's suffocating. The sky is empty, not even the colors of the sunset as the evening sky is stuck in a murky gray. There are no sheets of clouds to stare down at her and no puffs of white to reach up and grab. If Nova could fly, she would be lost in an endless void with nothing to look at—not even a sun.

Why does no one believe me? she cries silently as she thinks of what led her to the roof. It wasn't a single moment, but many pushing on top of each other until she cracked.

"Well, what do you want then?" her ex-boyfriend, Henry, asked after another short-lasting doctor's visit.

Not to be in pain, she thought but didn't say. She knew he wouldn't understand—the med student who saw the negative test results and essentially said, *Yay, you're not dying. We can go home now.* Was the pain gone? No. But it wasn't life-threatening, so Nova was supposed to be happy. She was told to be happy.

"The good news is that whatever is going on is not major enough to appear on any tests," the ER doctor said. "All we can do now is hope you find a way to manage the pain at home."

Nova heard this story before—where the doctors give up if the diagnosis is not easily ticked off in a handy little box. If they give up on her, should she do the same?

Nova lets her wrists dangle off the roof wall as she watches little people wrangle their children and command their dogs before the sun goes down completely. Her throat quivers as she holds back tears she doesn't want to cry. The tears came anyway.

"Have you considered psychotherapy?" another doctor had said. "Since nothing is coming up in the labs, it's probably just a mental manifestation—"

I'm not making this up, she thought while not listening to the doctor. If he wouldn't listen to her, why should she listen to him?

The last time she was at the hospital, she had prayed for appendicitis. She prayed for something to kill her because that would mean answers. That would mean one simple surgery to make it all go away—the doctor's scalpel a magical wand.

Nova has no magic in her life, and she knows now she never will.

With blurry vision, Nova looks back up to find something, anything, in the sky. Something to tell her she'll be okay. There is nothing but a cloudless sky.

Earlier that day, Nova threw a flower vase at Henry . . . something she had never done before. "Get out!" she screamed. Broken glass shined against the yellow kitchen light and brown water with moldy lilies spread throughout the floor. "Get out of here Henry."

"Why are you so angry?" Henry said. "I'm just trying to help you see the positive side. The labs said you're okay."

"You're just like all the doctors and I can't handle this anymore!" Nova's body took over as her fingers tightened and shook. Her breath vibrated uncontrollably, and she gasped for air as if she was drowning underwater. Suddenly, without the energy to stand, she curled into a ball on the floor and cried. Her hands were claws that cupped over her ears and she rocked back and forth.

"Nova—"

"You don't care about me!" she screamed at Henry. She knew it wasn't true, but it was enough to push him out the door. She wanted to be alone—to be free from the voices that said she deserved the pain.

"No, I do."

"No one cares about me!"

"The doctors did their best," Henry said. Nova didn't want to hear it. They could have done better.

"You don't care about me. You don't care about me. You don't care about me. You don't—" Nova continued to say the same sentence over and over again while she rocked back and forth.

Eventually, Henry left and slammed the door behind him. But when she was left alone, Nova did not stop rocking.

Nova pushes the memory out of her mind and looks for clouds she knows she'll never find. She scratches her head, sliding her finger through the thick matt coating her scalp. She twisted her hair in a bun the last time she went to the ER, and the thin pillow on the overly used hospital bed was the point of no return for Nova's hair. She never attempted to brush out her ridiculously long and thick locks since.

Twinkling lights hanging above the roof deck flash on as the sunlight says its final goodbye. Nova grabs the roof's waist-high wall, the unbearable pain returning. A headache in the stomach with a burning sharp stab is the best way she can describe it—a migraine with a knife on fire right under the ribs. *Right on schedule,* she thinks. The pain is always there; it may go away for twenty minutes or so, but it always comes back eventually. Her knees shake and her body weight makes her weak. If it wasn't for the wall, she surely would have met her face with the hard concrete floor. *I can't live like this anymore.*

Nova glances over to a nearby tree planter box—the perfect height for a step stool to get over the wall . . .

.

.

.

If only she had noticed that dark rain clouds shifted to reveal a bright, full moon that was pleading to her, *Don't jump.*

Bluebottles wash ashore because they are victims to the wind.
They don't even swim; they float and can only ride
the path the ocean creates for them.

When Mothers Fly

Briana

My mother was a soarer. In my eyes, she was a sky goddess because she could touch the sun; something that's only a faint memory now. When I was young, I would gaze up into the clouds and watch the wind brush her hair past her cheeks while her dress fluttered behind her ankles. That was, until, the sky went empty because my mother lost her flight.

Some light peeks through the thick plastic blinds covering our back sliding door, but the house is dim and cold. The news plays on the television as I yawn while half-listening to the news anchor. I pour some fresh coffee into my thermos, take a sip for quality inspection, and make my way out of the kitchen. I grab the remote to turn off the television but pause, watching the news like a dumbfounded child.

"Perry Pond, a small trailhead tucked away in a suburban neighborhood, has been purchased," the news anchor says.

I slump onto the couch and dangle the remote between my knees as I lean in closer to the television. The news fades in photos of Perry Pond, with sun sprinkling across the rich blue water. "Our pond," I whisper. I haven't been there in years—not since the accident. But that place . . . it was my entire childhood and the last time I saw my mother happy.

Perry Pond is a few blocks away from home, hidden behind large oak trees and surrounded by tall knee-scratching grass. It was our special spot, where my mother would give me a taste of what it felt like to fly. I couldn't contain my giggles when she would swim in the air above my head. My dainty fingers held tightly onto my mother's long bony ones, and her smile would gleam down at me as she flew above my head in circles.

My toes danced in the shallow pond and water splashed around me as I twirled underneath my mother's soars. My feet hovered slightly above the ground, the water rippling around me as my mother flew faster and soared higher. My cheeks ached from my laughter and my eyes sparkled as I watched my mother become haloed by the sun that shined behind her. I saw my mother touch the sky while I dangled underneath her. In that moment gravity didn't tether me to the ground; it was the closest I ever got to experiencing my mother's magic.

That was the time of my childhood I cherish the most; the memories impossible to forget and the moments I am desperate to relive. I don't know why my mother was gifted with flight, but I wasn't. I never thought it was fair.

When I was little, my mother loved to braid my hair. She made me sit on the floor in front of the couch while she made fun designs in my hair. A movie would play on the television, and I tried to watch the dancing teddy bears or singing flowers but my mother was not as gentle with her hair tugs as she thought she was.

"Keep your head still," she said as she repositioned my head.

When flying fairies fluttered across the screen, I thought back to our special moments at our pond.

"Mommy?" I asked. "Why can't I fly like you?"

I felt her shrug while she continued to braid my hair. "I don't know, sweetie."

"Will I ever be able to fly?"

She sighed slowly, releasing a long breath. The silence was uncomfortable, with only silly songs singing on the television, until my mother finally said, "You don't need to fly. You're already special."

I folded my arms and pouted. "But I still want to fly."

I don't even know where my mother's magic comes from—and I don't think my mother knows. It always felt like the universe was punishing me for something. Why else would I be cursed with having feet stuck on the ground . . . a curse I regretfully spread to my mother.

Memories of the accident rush into my mind, but I quickly shoo them away. I focus on the news broadcast and fight to keep away my tears.

"Construction will start shortly with plans to build a grocery store in its place," the news anchor says. They go on to report how the store will be good for the community, but I don't care. *They're going to rip up our pond?*

With the news still playing, I rush into my mother's room. "Mom!" I call down the hallway. "Mom!"

I don't bother knocking and instead just burst into the sunless room. Dark green curtains are shut over the bedroom windows, with not even a crack of light. I wince when I stub my toe on the corner of her bed and cautiously put my hands in front of me to feel where I am going.

I find the lump of her body under the blanket and sit down beside her. The room is quiet except for the squeak of the mattress and a hum from the vents. I shake my mother's shoulder as I say, "Mom, they're ripping up the pond."

Her head is buried in her pillow, but she lifts it slightly to say, "What?"

"Our pond. They're making it into a grocery store."

"Oh," she says, her voice muffled by her pillow. With that one word, I could hear her heartbreak. She's just as disappointed as I am.

"Let's go."

She does nothing, except her breath quickens.

"Let's go to the pond. Before the construction starts." While I wait for her answer, I dig my toes into the carpet and feel the floorboards with my nails.

I wait a bit to see if my mother answers, but I quickly lose my patience. "Please," I whine. "For old time's sake."

The woman lying beside me is a stranger now because that's what she wants. Her bed is not only her home but her life, and not even the loss of our special place is enough to get out of the sheets.

I sigh and get off the bed to bring light into the room. The metal curtain rings ding against the rod as I whip the heavy curtains open. Daylight bursts into the room and casts shadows on the bed in the shape of my mother's body. At the side of the room, next to the window, is a wheelchair. I unfold the chair and wheel it to my mother's bedside. "The weather's warm today," I say with hopeless optimism. "Feeling the sun on your cheeks might be nice."

My mother says nothing. She won't even look at me.

"I have a little time before I have to go to work."

Again, she says nothing.

I stomp my foot and bite my lip in frustration. "Please. At least get out of this room." I wait for a response but am only met with silence. "Mom," I bark. I wait, but she doesn't move an inch. I give up. "Fine," I finally say. "I guess the pond isn't that important."

I march out of the room and leave my mother to her silence, but I keep the curtains open. At least she won't spend the day in the dark.

Ginora

My heart chills in a bed of ice when I hear Briana slam the bedroom door. But I don't move. Instead, I close my eyes to shut out the world—snuff out all light beaming into my room—and force myself to go back to sleep. It is all I can do because when I am asleep my heartbreak finally rests.

But sleep doesn't last forever; as the sun beams into my bedroom, my body is wide awake. My gut turns to glass and twists into knives as a wheelchair stares me in the face. I look at it every day, in shadows and sunrays . . .

I used to be able to touch the stars and tickle the sun. But now, if I were to fly it would only be in my head. I was looked up to by my daughter and she was proud of me. That is all gone now that the sky is empty. And my daughter looks down at me.

I close my eyes and sink my head deeper into my pillow as I go back in time, to when we soared together at our pond. Back to when I was a good mother. Briana's laughter sings in my ears and I can feel her fragile, tiny hands in my mine. The wind rushes against my cheeks as my little girl dangles beneath me; I've never seen her happier.

A painful sting pierces my eyes. My brows clench together as I massage my palms; a poor attempt to stop tears. I miss seeing my daughter smile. I miss seeing her happy. Every day—as I sulk in the bed I'm trapped in—my daughter stands above me defeated. And I did that to her. I took away her happiness.

"I want to fly," Briana said when she was little. "Why can't I fly like you, Mommy?"

My body broke from the inside every time I heard her ask me why she couldn't fly because I never had an answer. My mother also couldn't fly. As far as I know, I'm the only one who can, or rather, could.

From the first second I became a mother, I tried to share my magic with my daughter. I helped her fly the best I could so she could experience the joy I wanted to give her. Her smile was blinding when she was a child, but I saw the smile disappear ever since I lost my flight. I can never again give her the joy she had when I could help her fly. That's why I can never look her in the eye; the pain behind her face is too unbearable to see.

I would break my back again if that meant she could be happy. But instead, I forced her to become a servant in her own home. A mother should care for her daughter and not the other way around.

I never realized how high our kitchen cabinets were until I was stuck in a chair. I was unable to reach the simplest things like salt and pepper.

"Mom, don't hurt yourself." Briana came rushing over when she saw me strain my arm as I tried to reach a place that was impossible to touch.

"I just need to get the—"

"No." Briana yanked my chair away from the counter and pushed me out of the kitchen. "I'll cook. You just find a movie to watch."

All I could do was watch movie after movie while Briana busied herself cooking recipes she didn't really know. Another movie while Briana untangled herself from a vacuum that was too heavy for me to handle while sitting. And a movie while Briana came home with a slouched back and baggy eyes from a job I know she hated. All the things I should be doing for her but couldn't anymore. And at night, I needed her help too.

"Hold onto my neck and I'll lift you," Briana said as she hunched over my chair.

I did as she said, held onto her tightly, and tried to make myself as light as possible. But I wasn't light enough. Her struggle was clear as she breathed heavily while lifting me in her arms to place me into the bed.

"Goodnight," Briana said out of breath.

Her face looked defeated with tired eyes. I saw the pain behind them as she looked at me. And I did that to her. I stopped watching movies and instead watched my bedroom window. I stopped leaving my bed and didn't get in my chair. I saved her from having to hurt herself just to help me—and I saved myself from watching her freedom be taken away.

And with the pond now being destroyed . . . it's just another thing I've taken away from Briana. I can't bear to look at how broken she is and I know if I were to speak, I would start crying. That's why I didn't say anything this morning. That's why I hardly say anything at all.

I bury my face in my mattress, ashamed of the life I pushed Briana into, and cry all my heartbreak out of my body. It's the only thing I have to pass the time.

Briana

When my office clock says 5 PM, I beeline for the exit. But when I'm outside on the curb, the rush is gone. I take my sweet time walking home, with slow and heavy steps. As I walk, I look up to the sky and count the colors in the clouds: grey, blue, white, and some pink swarm over each other in a fight for glory. The clouds overlap and entangle themselves as they swallow the sky whole. I watch the clouds do their dance all the way home, but I stall on the porch. I don't want to go inside, where the walls suffocate me while my mother lives in darkness.

So, I decide to go to the pond . . . without my mother. As I hike through the high brush, my gut twists with guilt. This is the first time I'm going to our secret place without her; it feels wrong.

A sharp knife carves out my stomach and stabs my heart like a pin cushion when I find a dried-out pond enclosed by a chain-link fence. Construction had already begun; the beautiful oasis is now just dirt and weeds. The pond is no longer a pond.

I let myself fall and dig my knees into the dirt. I know it's not my fault our special pond is gone, but it still feels like it is. Everything always ends up being my fault.

I still remember the night when the rain echoed louder than the thunder and the lightning whipped trees. The grey streets were tinted blue, and the sky was black despite it being midday. I got my driver's license earlier that day and stole my mother's car to celebrate—not knowing about the storm. During the worst of it, in the high winds and heavy rains, I was stalled at the side of the road several miles away from home. No buses were running, and no cars could make it down the flooded streets.

"Mom?" I cried on the phone. "I'm stuck in the storm."

"Where are you?" she said.

"The corner of Melva and Roe."

"Stay right there," she said without missing a beat. "I'm coming to get you."

I don't know how long I sat waiting, but it was long enough to be shivering in a car that wouldn't start while the wind whooshed against the windows. In the distance, I could see a small orb of light fly towards me. The orb was blurry behind all the rain, but it grew larger and brighter until I realized it was my mother in the sky holding a flashlight. I got out of the car and let myself get drenched in the rain.

In the sky, lightning struck behind my mother; the light reflected off the falling rain and flashed a blue outline around her body. My breath tightened when I watched her fly amongst lightning, but she didn't look scared. Instead, she stared down at me with worried eyes.

"Are you okay?" she asked.

"I'm sorry," I called out, my voice raised to hear myself in the rain. "Sorry I'm making you fly in this storm."

"That doesn't matter." My mother hovered over my head and reached her arm out towards me. "Let's get you somewhere safe."

I nodded my head, but before I had a chance to grab her hand a flash of light rang louder than a gunshot as thunder and lightning struck at the same time. It was deafening and blinding; a moment where your life flashed before your eyes. The next thing I knew, my mother collapsed on the ground being swallowed by the flood. The snap of her back was louder than any thunder crack, and she has been paralyzed ever since.

The sky burns red as the sun slowly falls behind the large pit of dirt that used to be the pond. The sunset is quick and before long I am engulfed by moonlight with no stars to count. Despite the glowing moon, the night sky is dark. Fitting.

I bury my face in my hands and cry, "I'm sorry." My shoulders shake from my tears and my head pounds. "I'm sorry I hurt you—"

My voice trails out as I realize I'm apologizing to no one. Alone at the destroyed pond, I know I need to speak those words to my mother. They are words I've been dreading, words I've never wanted her to hear, but words I have to say. I've already lost our special place, and I don't want to lose her too.

Ginora

I don't have to open my eyes to know Briana is home. The click of light switches echo through the thin walls and her steps down the hallway are heavy, like always. Even as a little girl she would clomp wherever she went, as if she was afraid to walk a little softer or stand a little taller.

My body tenses as I brace myself for her gentle knock—but it never comes. Instead, the door creaks and feet shuffle on the carpet. The mattress rises as I feel a weight on the other side of the bed. Something is different; this is not how the routine goes. When Briana got home from work, she would knock, peek her head in to say hello, and then start dinner. But tonight, there is no knock. No hello. We lay together for a few moments with only the hallway light bleeding into the room.

"Mom," Briana says quickly, finally breaking the silence. "We need to talk."

I slowly turn my head and see my daughter lying on her back—her eyes counting the spots on the ceiling and her fingers interlocking on top of her stomach.

"Briana?"

She sighs and turns her head towards me, but she doesn't look at me. She looks past me at the window that shows a moon strangled by rain clouds. Normally I am the one too afraid to look at her, but now it was the opposite as I urge her to look at me. Either way, we always seem to miss each other's gaze.

"I'm sorry," Briana whispers as she watches the sun disappear. Her voice is soft and barely heard. It wobbles and cracks—and I hear an intense pain behind those two simple words. But what does she have to be sorry about? It is I who should be apologizing.

"Don't—" I start to say.

"No," she snaps. She gets up abruptly and sits crisscross on the bed. Her back is hunched, and her hands are buried in the crease of her knees. "I have to say this before I lose my courage."

I say nothing as I lie stiff on my bed. I look at her knee resting on top of my foot, but I can't feel it. I count four cricket chirps before Briana speaks again.

Briana shoves her face in her hands as she cries. Her shoulders shake and her head bobs. It's excruciating to watch her. I try to reach out to hug her, but she's sitting just out of reach. "I'm sorry I did this to you," she cries. "I'm a terrible daughter."

My throat sinks to my toes and my fingers vibrate with devastation. I can't believe what I'm hearing. I never thought of Briana as a terrible daughter. I never thought she was to blame—

I sink further into the mattress when I realize my actions led her to believe just that. I avoided her, I shut her out . . . of course she thought those awful things.

"Briana," I say, my motherly voice taking over. "Don't you dare think that—"

"It's true—"

"No." I use my arms to lift my body and scoot closer to her. I grab her chin and force her to look up at me. "You are the most wonderful daughter any mother could ask for. I am the one who needs to apologize to you."

"But the storm—"

"Never mind the storm."

Briana rips her face out of my hand. "How can you say that?! I'm the reason you lost your flight! I'm the reason you had to come rescue me. You got hurt because of me!"

"Is that what this is about? Briana." I sigh. "I have never blamed you for that. It's my job to protect you come rain or shine."

"Then why shut me out?" She cries and I didn't think my heart could break even more.

"Because I was ashamed." I begin crying too. "You used to be so happy. I couldn't bring you happiness anymore. I watched you be sad every day and . . . " My voice trails out as I realize how selfish I am. "I just couldn't bear it. I couldn't watch you having to take care of me. I thought if I stayed in here," I take a deep breath. "If I stayed in bed at least I could save you from having to carry me in and out of my chair."

"Mom," Briana snaps. "Being shut out sucks."

My head suddenly feels heavy, and the pillow sounds too good right now.

"I don't mind helping you," Briana continues. "It's the least I could do since I destroyed your life."

I scoff. "You didn't—"

"Didn't I though? Mom, you can't walk. Let alone you lost your magic."

My breath quickens and as I talk, my tone becoming harsh. "I don't care about losing my magic. I care about losing the one thing I had to make you happy."

"No," Briana cries. Her mouth gapes and her eyes are glossy. "No. That's not right. I wasn't happy because you could fly. I was happy being with you. I was happy to see how amazing my mother was. And I thought I was the reason why I lost that." It's difficult to hear her words behind her tears. "I was why I lost my mother."

My mouth dries and it's painful to swallow. I let my daughter believe I hated her because I pushed her away. And there's nothing I could do to make up for that. But now, maybe I could—?

"You didn't lose me," I say urgently. "I'm here."

I reach out for a hug, terrified she won't return it. My heart burns with relief when she falls into my arms and hugs me tightly. We cry on each other's shoulders for what seems like hours.

Eventually, I finally say, "Do you want to go on a walk tomorrow? We can find a new pond."

Briana leans back and the smile I have missed finally returns.

Under Water

Deep underwater, dark shadows engulfed nearly everything as they crept in from every which way. That was, until, pools of sunlight cut through the water; bright radiant strips speared down and sliced through the shadows. Water ripples sparkled like diamonds, but the light didn't last long as the shadows caved in once again until there was nothing left but gloom underwater.

Penelope floated on her back, stuck under the murky water. Her fingertips, nimble and thin, reached to escape the water prison—but she was too deep. Her limbs were frozen, unable to swim for a reprieve, and she sank deeper into a cold abyss. Her long, caramelized brown hair danced against her cheeks like dainty feathers. The deeper she sank, the more water filled her lungs—and the more Penelope forgot what it felt like to breathe. White silk brushed up against her arms like a gentle stroke from a fearful painter; the long flowing gown she wore swam around her in a cloud-like form preparing for a heavy rain. Deeper she drowned with all radiance gone.

Penelope gasped for air and her eyes shot open so fast they nearly popped out of her skull. The old, stiff mattress squeaked as she sat up and her back sprang up straight. Her right hand was planted flat on her chest as she attempted to steady her breathing.

That felt so real, Penelope thought.

She took deep, raspy breaths as she studied her small studio apartment and tried to place herself back into reality. She gazed at her beige carpet, which had a few grey spots, and remembered how it felt rough and scratchy. Every day, it was like walking barefoot in a poorly funded church while simultaneously receiving an oddly satisfying foot rub. Any food crumbs present were invisible and surprisingly unnoticeable, but they were still there nonetheless.

Penelope let her eyes wander to the little trinkets she had scattered around. There was a wooden rose paperweight on the bedside table with red sparkles on its pedals; it was a gift her mom gave her when she graduated high school. She glanced at the shimmering ceramic palm-sized llama on the windowsill; her mom loved to gift random and cute things for Easter. And she stared on top of her bookshelf at the porcelain bulldog cookie jar Penelope made at *Color Me Mine* with her mom.

Her skin was chilled deeply with an invisible ice; goosebumps and stick-straight hair cluttered her body. She closed her eyes briefly and quickly found herself floating deep underwater into the unknown again. It felt as if water ripples were brushing up against her, and she swayed softly on her mattress. Had she never woken up from her dream, or was she trapped in a nightmare?

Like a seamless waterfall, her body fell limp onto her mattress and her head buried deeply into her pillow. She was ready to embrace sleep but there was a loud and sudden music of twinkling stars. Penelope groaned and wasted no time turning off her alarm.

"Crap," she whispered as she looked at the time and realized she had class in less than thirty minutes—but the cocoon in her bed-sheets was too inviting. A million thoughts beat against her mind each second.

I could slip back into sleep and pretend my alarm never went off.

Lateness was inevitable so what was the point in going?

Would anyone even notice if I wasn't there?

Yet, deep in her heart she knew none of those thoughts were the right answer. *Don't give up what you truly want, for what you want in the moment,* she remembered her mom saying time and time again.

"This is for you Mom," Penelope said to the ceiling before she pulled herself out of bed. She had already missed four classes this semester and a fifth absence was an automatic fail. Her mom would be rolling in her still-fresh grave if Penelope flunked out of college. She already missed a few weeks of school; she hadn't gone to class since the funeral. But today was the day she was supposed to go back. Apparently, two weeks of mourning is plenty.

Penelope didn't bother changing out of her pajamas, nor did she even brush her hair. She was only one student in a sea of others after all. Before she made her way out of the door, she stopped quickly in the bathroom to apply deodorant. She didn't care if she looked like a goblin, but she didn't want to smell like one too.

As she reached for the little blue stick on her bathroom counter, her wrist brushed against an orange prescription bottle and it dropped to the floor. When she picked up the bottle, she briefly scanned the label before twisting the white lid and swallowing a pill.

"This will help you with your grief," her doctor had said as he wrote the prescription.

Penelope swallowed her first pill shortly after her mom's funeral, but it didn't make her feel better. So, she took another one . . . and another . . . and another until she felt the pain slip away. She grabbed the orange bottle, put it in her backpack, and headed out the door.

It did not take long for Penelope to arrive on campus, but she couldn't stop her chest from tightening when she got there. The last time she was there, her mom hugged her goodbye and wished her luck on her midterms. The hallways of the community college were small, and she was lost in a crowd of strangers. No one made eye contact with her, even though she aimlessly looked at all of them. They ignored her; she was essentially invisible. There was a brush against her shoulder, a step on her shoe, and she had to squeeze between chatting bodies that blocked the only pathway. No one batted an eye as she walked past. No one even noticed she was there. Penelope couldn't help but walk slower—with a heavier step and fallen shoulders. Her nearly matted hair naturally fell over her eyes like an emo middle school girl using every desperate attempt to hide her identity.

Her thin-soled shoes scratched against the patterned carpet that belonged in an 80's arcade. The more weight her feet placed into the ground, the more heat she radiated into her arches. She walked down the hallway with a leash tugging her backwards; school was the last place she wanted to be.

"Hey, Penelope!" a distant voice called. "Penelope!"

But Penelope didn't notice. Instead, she kept walking with her head hung low until she got to her classroom. Luckily, the class was in the lecture theatre with a hundred seats. Penelope chose the seat in the back closest to the door—grateful that in this class she could easily hide.

"Penelope," a girl out of breath said. "Did you not see me waving at you?"

Penelope looked up to see What's-Her-Bucket from her study group. What's-Her-Bucket climbed over Penelope's leg to grab the seat next to her.

"Did you do the reading?" What's-Her-Bucket asked.

Penelope shook her head, not making eye contact.

"Oh, why not?"

Penelope shrugged.

"What," What's-Her-Bucket chuckled, "cat got your tongue?"

Penelope didn't react. She didn't do anything. Actually, no. She did do something. She, as secretly as she could, snuck into her backpack and popped another pill. The day was harder than she thought it would be.

It didn't take long for class to start—thank goodness—and everyone pulled out their notebooks or laptops to frantically write down every word the professor said. Everyone, that is, except for Penelope. She just sat there and listened to the AC that struggled to do its job.

"Holistic medicine is the only right way to do healthcare," the professor said. "Do you know why? *Drugs.*"

Penelope lifted her head and started listening to the lecture.

"Other medical professionals rely on prescribing medication to their patients because it's the easy way out. But do you know what happens when your entire treatment plan is medication?"

Penelope slouched and her breath quickened.

"It doesn't fix anything. It's just a band-aid. Temporary and eventually useless," the professor said, his tone harsh and cold. "And what's worse, the patient becomes reliant. And let me tell you—" He used his fat finger to firmly point at every single student in the class. "You should never rely on prescription drugs. It's not smart."

Penelope's fast breathing turned into hyperventilation until she had no breath left. All the while, her prescription bottle burned a hole in her backpack. Yes, she was dumb. She was stupid. Her professor said so.

I can't do this, she thought and rushed out of the classroom. *I'm sorry Mom.*

While running out of the building, she somehow ran into every shoulder and collided with every single body. Hot tears ran down her cheeks and her breath was raspy as she forgot how to breathe. *Stupid,* she thought all the way home.

Once home and alone, Penelope thought the only thing she could do was run a bath. Her mom would always say, "There's nothing a nice warm bath can't cure." She listened to the running water, like a gushing bomb with a never-ending flame. The spout splashed water into the filling tub, drowning out every other sound in the world.

She sat on the edge of the tub and let her body sway to the melody of the waterspout. Her mind was numb—fogged to the point that any thought was too painful to bear. So, she shut off her mind and just swayed against the bathtub's edge.

That was until she felt a cold sensation soak her bathrobe. She glanced down behind her and gasped when she saw the tub overflowing with water. Frantically, she turned off the waterspout and sighed as she heard the bathtub's draining mechanism start up.

Thank goodness for the overflow drain, she thought.

She just stared at the water for a minute and intensely listened to single droplets from the spout ping against the full tub. She let the sound mesmerize her for way too long before she slipped out of her bathrobe, dropped it onto the dirty floor, and crawled into the welcoming water. In the tub, she couldn't help but notice the mess she was bathing in. The bathtub glued to a tiled wall was supposed to be white. It was supposed to shine with a clean glisten. Instead, it was grimy with a gray dirt . . . no shine and no glimmer. At least, the water was warm.

The lightbulb stuck behind a dust-coated ceiling fishbowl flickered; the bathroom was lit very dimly like a dancing candle flame for a few seconds until the room exploded with a blinding light for another second or two. It was an endless cycle. With closed eyes, it wasn't difficult to imagine a raging party with strobe lights inside the little nook bathroom.

Penelope tried to drift into nothingness as she soaked her body in bath water—but the nothingness never came. No matter how much she tried, she couldn't turn off her thoughts.

I miss Mom.

The only person who cared for me died.

I'm alone. Alone forever.

I have no one.

Her thoughts were overwhelming as her heart cried.

"Why did you have to leave me, Mom?" she whimpered to the ceiling light. "Why didn't you tell me you were sick? Why—"

Penelope lifted her knees and burrowed her nose in her kneecaps. "Why do I have to be alone?" she said, her voice muffled by her skin.

She sat there, curled and hunched over until she went limp. She laid back, shut her eyes, and rested her head against the tile wall. Eventually, she slipped deeper into the tub and fully submerged herself fully underwater. All that was left above the water was her nose—and she breathed in deeply.

Would anyone even notice if I disappeared? she thought.

Without another thought, Penelope dunked her nose in the water and wondered how long she could stay under. 1 . . . 2 . . . 3 . . . all she did was count seconds; she had no choice because her swarming thoughts were a dangerous storm that no one could handle. Her eyes were still closed as she forced herself to stay under the water.

Penelope found herself floating deep underwater again, in murky shadows, with a white gown flowing around her arms. Her back was arched as she floated in stillness, drowning. She sank deeper, and water filled her lungs. She was engulfed by darkness with all light swallowed by underwater shadows of emptiness.

The fabric of her white gown brushed against her forearms as she reached for the surface. She expected to be too deep for a reprieve, but when her fingertip felt the cold air from the surface—she was shocked. Sunlight shot streams into the water, causing glittering streaks to shimmer throughout. The bright radiance was blinding, and the dark shadows crept backward. The darkness was retreating. The darkness was losing. How could this be?

She was floating alone underwater, surrounded by pools of sunlight that connected to the heavens. Water sparkled all around her, with no signs of the dark shadows. It was just her and the light in an underwater sanctuary.

Penelope yanked herself out from underneath the bath water. She coughed and gagged, gasping for air as she sat, cold in her lonely bathtub. Her dream had returned, exactly how it was before. Only this time, it was a different ending. She combed shaking fingers through her wet hair. Was she meant to escape the underwater depths? Inside, Penelope thought the answer was no.

Her body was frozen with shock, fear, and something else she couldn't identify. A chill ran up her spine, down her arms, into her neck, and through her knees. She looked down at the tiny pool she sat in and wondered if she should slip under again. She pulled her knees to her chest and hung on for dear life. Her body twitched while she rested her chin on her kneecaps. Her eyes remained open, but they weren't looking at anything. They were blank.

Penelope watched her feet soak in the water and wondered if it was possible to drown in a bathtub. She shook her head, scared of her own thoughts.

Get out, she told her thoughts. *Get out.*

But she couldn't get the idea of drowning off her mind. The more she thought about it, the more she considered it.

"I can't handle this," she cried to no one. With shaking fingers, she reached for her phone that she left on top of the nearby toilet.

Please answer, she silently pleaded. *I need my sister.*

Tears crept into Penelope's eyes when the rings stopped. It only rang three times, which meant the call was declined.

She called again, but this time she only got one ring.

Her tears burned her cheeks when she called again. "Come on, come on, come on," she cried. "Please answer."

No answer. Directly to voicemail.

"Robin!" she screamed into her phone.

Panic rose in her throat as she continued to call just to get a robot voice that said, "We're sorry but *Robin Evana* is not unavailable."

"Robin," Penelope cried, her voice echoing. "Please." She lowered her head until her forehead touched the tip of the water. "I don't want to be alone anymore."

Penelope called ten more times before she gave up. "Stupid," she said. "I'm so stupid. Why would I think she would want to talk to me?"

Penelope hadn't spoken to her sister since the funeral, and before that they only spoke when it was Christmas or someone's birthday. Sometimes she had a three-way call with Robin and her mom when they both happened to call Mom at the same time. Mom was always the liaison that got the sisters chatting with each other. And when Mom died, the chatting stopped. Robin was very busy apparently and had no time for her baby sister.

I can't live like this anymore, she thought.

Penelope's orange prescription bottle she had left on the counter caught her eye. *I'll see you soon Mom.*

It may sound silly, but bluebottles saved my sister and me.

She's a Bluebottle

Water ripples reflected onto the stone-like floor as Robin walked through a tunnel of glass. She kept her chin tall and shoulders stern, ignoring the bulging fisheyes that watched her from every angle. A manta ray glided above her head while her heels clicked on the floor with each step. "As you can see," she said in her fake *I'm-so-good-at-my-job* voice, "our sea tunnel gives you an immersive aquarium experience. The glass is so clear, you're basically scuba diving without getting wet." She hated that line, but her boss made her say it.

Her boss made her do a lot of things now. She shouldn't be doing these tours; she should be in the lab studying her jellyfish, conducting research, and caring for the unfortunate ones who got sick. She was a marine biologist, not a pretty face to show off fish to children.

The sea tunnels stretched for what felt like miles while little kids yelled "I see Dory" or "There's Nemo." Robin walked stiffly and poised in front of the tour group, and her stomach fluttered with a pleasant tingle when she reached the jellyfish room, the end of the tour.

"And this," she swept her arms around the room for people to gaze at the darkly painted blue walls that had peep windows into jellyfish tanks, "is our jellyfish room. Did you know there's more than one type of jellyfish?"

Robin pointed to a back corner of the room and said, "Over there are blue blubber jellyfish." She walked along the wall until she was next to a tank window with an extravagant blue frame. "And over here are my favorite, the bluebottle jellyfish," she said. Little kids shoved their way up the front of the group and got on their tippy toes to stare at a clump of jellyfish that looked like sacks of blue dye. "Interestingly, bluebottle jellyfish are *technically* not jellyfish. They are a zooid—or a colony of individuals that need each other to live. They cannot survive on their own. Together, they use their tentacles to catch, sting, and kill their prey."

Seeing the kids get excited by the bluebottles warmed Robin's heart. As much as she hated doing tours, she loved this part. She was not much older than their age when she got fascinated by bluebottles. It was a weird thing for a kid to be passionate about, but Robin loved learning about jellyfish.

When the tour was over, she guided her group to exit through the gift shop and was about to make her way to her office when a deep voice stopped her.

"Robin Evana?"

Robin turned to see a group of four old, white men dressed in black suits and ties that were too tight around their necks. "Yes?" she answered sheepishly.

"My name is Fredrick Bowlin, the Chairman of the aquarium's Board of Directors." He swept a hand to gesture to the other men. "And these are my colleagues who also serve on the board."

Robin's gut clenched as she reached out to shake his hand. "Oh, yes. Nice to meet you." She had never met a member of the board before, let alone four of them all at once. Why the board was here she had no clue, but her gut said it wasn't good.

"We, unfortunately, have to make significant budget cuts due to profits being down," Fredrick said. "The program we're currently considering defunding is the jellyfish, specifically the bluebottles."

Her breath hitched. Jellyfish were her whole job; if they were to defund it . . . Robin's breath quickened, and she tried her best to hide her panic.

"Since you're the resident jellyfish specialist, we thought it best for you to show us around the facility before we make our final decision," Fredrick said. "We'd like to see your research specifically."

"Of course," Robin squeaked. She took a deep breath and guided the board to her research lab hidden in the back of the aquarium.

In her lab, she pulled out every manila folder she could find that had printed documents of her current research. She showed them the data she had collected and the work she had done with the city to preserve jellyfish life on the beaches.

The board nodded their heads but said nothing. Robin tried to make herself forget that her job was on the line as she led them to the tanks that housed the sick jellyfish. When she was about to explain her process of nursing them back to health, a ringtone of an annoying and all-too-common marimba echoed throughout the room. Robin gave a sheepish smile and breathed, "My apologies." She briskly pulled out her phone and silenced it. Before placing it back into her pocket, she paused to read the caller's name: *Penelope.*

Robin thought nothing of the call and continued conducting the tour of the jellyfish facilities. She'd call her sister back later. She got two sentences in before her pocket buzzed. Robin ignored it, pretended her phone did not exist, and continued telling the board about her research. Relief spread through her chest when the buzzing finally stopped, but the calm was brief.

Buzz, buzz, buzz—again.

She reached into her pocket and pressed a button to stop the vibrating. "Bluebottle lifespans at this aquarium are—"

Buzz, buzz, buzz.

Silenced.

Buzz, buzz, buzz.

Silenced.

"I'm sorry. Give me a moment," Robin said, trying her best to hide her frustration. She pulled out her phone and turned it off completely. Whatever Penelope was calling for wasn't important enough to lose her job.

The workday was finally over, and Robin was ready to crash into bed. She was told the board would make their final decision by next week. That gave her seven full days to stew and wonder if she would be out of a job. As she walked to her car, Robin remembered all of Penelope's phone calls. *I should call her back,* she thought. She pulled out her phone and nearly dropped it when she saw fourteen missed calls. "Geez Pen. What is all this?"

Robin rolled her eyes as she dialed her sister's number. It rang out for a while until she got voicemail. She tried calling one more time, but it was the same. She was ready to shrug it off and say, *If it's important she'll call back,* but her stomach told her to drive to Penelope's apartment.

I haven't talked to her in a while, she thought. *It might be nice to see her.*

Robin drummed her fingers against her steering wheel as she tried to remember how to get to Penelope's apartment. She remembered Penelope's apartment building as a little kooky; it was a rectangular brick house cut into fourths. Three apartments were on the ground level, but one—Penelope's—was in the basement. But she couldn't recall anything else, like how to get there.

After combing through her old text messages, she eventually found Penelope's address and backed out of the aquarium's parking lot. The drive to Penelope's neighborhood was shorter than what Robin expected. She turned onto her sister's street but tensed when she saw bright flashing blue and red lights.

"Uh-oh," she whispered.

She slowed down to observe the situation, thinking a house had been robbed or something. When she realized the police and ambulance were parked outside Penelope's apartment, panic rushed in. And when a group of paramedics wheeled a girl out on a stretcher—her heart froze.

Robin scratched the side of her car against the curb when she parked on the street. She rushed out of the car and ran to get a closer look. It was hard to tell at first, but when her heels sunk into the grass she recognized the girl on the stretcher as Penelope.

"Penelope?!" she screamed as she ran to the stretcher.

A strong and burly paramedic held her back.

She hit him in the shoulder frantically to push him off. "Let me go!" she cried. "That's my sister!" She looked around the paramedic's thick body and watched Penelope get loaded into the ambulance. "Pen! Penelope!"

"Ma'am, please stay calm," the paramedic said.

"What happened?!"

"We got a 911 call about an overdose."

Robin's body went numb, and she had to lean into the paramedic to keep her balance. It felt as though she was standing outside naked in the middle of winter and her vision became a watercolor painting where the colors ran along the page, drowned in water. Objects, people, lights . . . everything was smeared in diagonal lines.

"We're taking her to the hospital," the paramedic said. "Do you want to ride with your sister?"

Robin urgently nodded and let the paramedic guide her into the back of the ambulance. During the drive to the hospital, the sirens were not as deafening as she thought they'd be—but that was only because something else smothered her mind.

Buzz, buzz, buzz.

Penelope's endless phone calls. Why didn't she answer the phone?

Buzz, buzz, buzz. It was all Robin could hear as she walked into the hospital, as nurses guided her to a waiting area, as she waited, and as the doctor told her Penelope was on suicide watch. *Buzz, buzz, buzz.*

"Luckily, we caught it early so it can be flushed out of her system," the doctor said. "Good thing you called 911 when you did."

"I—I didn't call," Robin said quietly, still in shock. "I wasn't there."

"Was someone else home?"

Robin shook her head. "No. She lives alone." As she spoke, she felt herself falling down a deep well where her voice echoed against dark walls. The word alone echoed the loudest.

The doctor nodded silently before he said, "She should be waking up soon. I'll send a psychologist to come talk to you."

The next few hours at the hospital were a blur. Many people came in to talk to her, but although they walked in at different times all Robin remembered was one colossal monster with a growling voice that said *Suicide Watch.*

When the monster was gone and the hospital room was eerily quiet—except for Penelope's faint breathing—Robin had nothing to do except twiddle her thumbs. She squeezed her fingertips until she felt pain, not knowing what she should do.

"Robin?" Penelope said weakly. Her eyes were barely open, fighting against the bright lights.

"Penelope." Robin scooted her chair closer to the hospital bed.

"You're here?" Penelope said.

"Of course I'm here. What were you thinking?"

The next words Penelope said broke Robin's heart. "I didn't want to be alone anymore."

Robin felt herself shrinking in her chair. A black hole grew underneath her and shrunk her lungs. "I'm sorry." Robin was barely able to speak. She swallowed down her tears and told herself she wasn't allowed to cry. She was supposed to be the strong, older sister. Tears wouldn't help Penelope now.

"Why didn't you answer the phone? Do you hate me that much?"

"No, no." Robin grabbed Penelope's hand and squeezed it. "I don't hate you. I was busy at work."

"You ignored me." Penelope pouted. "You can't even answer a damn phone call."

"I'm sorry. I had an intense day at work and would have lost my job if I answered the phone. I called you back . . . " Robin's voice trailed off. "But it was too late."

The silence in the room was heavy, enough to crack the floor. That was, until Penelope finally mumbled, "I changed my mind."

Robin tilted her head closer to her sister, unsure what was just said. "What?"

"I changed my mind. Right after I took the pills, I changed my mind." Penelope's face was drowned by her tears. Her voice wobbled and was barely audible, but Robin still understood every word. "Mom wouldn't have wanted me to. I wanted to take it back, so I called 911."

"You called them yourself?"

Penelope nodded.

Robin hugged Penelope, as best as she could on the hospital bed. "I'm so glad you did. I don't want you to go."

Penelope pushed Robin away. "Then why don't you talk to me?" she spat. Her eyes narrowed and she looked both angry and sad.

Robin leaned back. "Work is . . . I'm the only caretaker for the jellyfish and they make me do tours now too. I've got a lot going on right now."

"Yeah, yeah," Penelope said with an eye roll. "Your job is more important than me."

Without any hesitation, Robin said, "That's going to change."

"What?"

Robin squeezed Penelope's shoulders. "That's going to change. I promise you, I will be a better sister. If you call me, I will answer. If I get fired, I don't care anymore. I didn't realize how much I was risking by prioritizing work."

"Do you really mean that?" Penelope kept her eyes pointed downward, as if she was afraid to meet Robin's gaze.

"I can't lose you too, Penelope. I've already lost Mom."

"I lost Mom too!" Penelope cried. "She was the only one who cared for me."

"That's not true—"

"It took me almost dying for you to care about me."

Robin opened her mouth to speak, but she didn't know what to say. There was nothing she could say.

"I needed you, Robin," Penelope cried. "I *needed* you."

This time, Robin couldn't stop her tears. "I need you, too."

"Then why do you ignore me?"

"I don't mean to—"

Penelope cut Robin off. "But you do! We don't talk, hang out, or do sister stuff. Why?"

"Because you're right!" Robin put her face in her hands, ashamed. "I didn't know I needed you until you almost died." Her shoulders shook as she cried; she wailed for a minute or two before she sniffed away her sadness and wiped her eyes with her knuckles. "You know what, I've been getting pretty lonely on Sundays. It's my day off. We could make that our sister day."

Penelope sat up a little straighter in her hospital bed and smiled. "You mean that?"

Robin nodded. "I want you in my life," she whispered.

"I want you too," Penelope whispered back.

Robin reached over and hugged her sister tightly. She never wanted to let go.

It had only been a day since Penelope called 911—she was still at the hospital. Robin went to bed that night with tears soaking her pillow and nightmares crowding her mind. The memories of the paramedics, the ambulance, and the doctors played a marathon as she slept. And when she woke, her tears never dried.

She didn't want to go to work, but she didn't have any PTO or sick days left; she used them all for her mom's funeral. Her heels clicked against the aquarium floor, like always, but this time the sound burned her ears. "Hello," she said as she approached a school field trip group of children and teachers. She stretched her face into a fake smile, but it only felt painful. "Are you ready to tour the aquarium?"

"YES!" little kids screamed.

Robin went through the tour like usual and did her best to bury her emotions. When she entered the jellyfish room, she sighed in relief. The tour was almost done, and then she could call to check in on Penelope.

"These are bluebottle jellyfish." Robin's voice was low; no matter how hard she had tried during the tour, she couldn't speak with the enthusiasm she was supposed to. "Interesting enough, bluebottle jellyfish are not jellyfish. They are a zooid—or a colony of individuals that need each other to live—" Robin paused and stared blankly at the bluebottles that floated around with bliss in an empty void of water. "They cannot survive on their own," she said, choking on her own words.

It was then that Robin realized Penelope was a bluebottle; she needed her sister to survive. *Maybe we're all bluebottles,* she thought.

We Are All Bluebottles

Support is out there so you never have to deal with things alone. Please seek help if you or someone you know feels in danger.

International Association for Suicide Prevention

www.iasp.info/suicidalthoughts

Call or text Suicide and Crisis Lifeline: 988 or text Crisis Text Line: "HOME" to 741-741

National Eating Disorders Association

www.nationaleatingdisorders.org

Online resources are available to learn about eating disorders and find treatment.

National Alliance on Mental Illness

www.nami.org/support-education/nami-helpline

Call 1-800-950-6264, text "Friend" to 62640, or email helpline@nami.org

It's never too late to get help and survive.

Afterword

This book, believe it or not, is autofiction. Some of it is true and some of it is not—but you don't get to know which is which. It's difficult writing about the truth, but it's the hard parts of life that need to be written about. We all deal with trauma. We all struggle. We all connect and disconnect with family. We all need to feel like we're not alone.

Before I began writing this book, I had no clue what a bluebottle was. I never thought there would be symbolism from a jellyfish, but now I connect everything to bluebottles. I am a bluebottle; I slip into dark thoughts and explore my darkest fantasies when I feel I can't talk to anyone. Yes, I have people who care for me that would have open ears, but the fear of judgment and embarrassment stops me (and so many of us) from speaking up. Sometimes, it's easier to keep everything inside.

And that is when I write. Writing lets out all the things I wish I was brave enough to say. I imagine what life could have been if it turned for the worse or what life could become if it turns for the better. Some of the truth in my stories is small—they are more fiction than autobiographical—but other stories are close to memoir where all I changed was the outcome.

Even though most of the stories in *Under Water* are based on true thoughts or experiences, this afterword is the most vulnerable I am being with you (my reader). I am not hiding behind fiction where I can tweak the truth, tell lies, and create a different universe. I am being honest with you here because bluebottles support each other. To help you, I am sharing my story—all of my stories—so you can be brave and speak up too. It's the hardest things that need to be talked about the most. And remember, you are not alone.

Diana Elizabeth Clarke

Diana Elizabeth Clarke is a creative writer, artist, and book designer. Her goal is to bring the world unique and impactful stories that will make a lasting impression on readers. She has a Master of Fine Arts in Creative Writing & Publishing Arts from The University of Baltimore and a Bachelor of Science in English with a Creative Writing Emphasis from Utah Valley University.

Diana's writing focuses on Weatherlore, a literary criticism and technique she developed that pays close attention to weather imagery and its metaphorical elements. She writes women-focused literary fiction and fantasy, looking to nature and her family for inspiration. In addition to writing, Diana shares a passion for dance. She began dancing at the age of eight and had a career in modern, contemporary, and ballet from 2015 to 2020. She also co-founded FUSE: A Festival of Dance, Poetry, and Prose in 2019, which was a three-day festival that encouraged dancers and writers to collaborate with each other.

Today, she draws from her previous experiences and present life to develop new stories she feels the world needs to hear. She currently works as a Professor of Writing at the University of Baltimore and was recently the Managing Editor of Plork Press. In her free time, you can find her obsessing over Disney Dreamlight Valley and cuddling with her dog, Nala.

Learn more about the author by visiting her website:

dianaelizclarke.wixsite.com/writer

Other Works by
Diana Elizabeth Clarke

"The Moment She Was Better"
Welter, Spring 2024 Issue, 2024

"Dead Hearts"
Warp & Weave, Volume 18 Issue 2, 2020

"I Was A Ballerina"
Touchstones: Journal of Literature & Art, Volume 32 Issue 2, 2020

"The Masquerade Killer"
Warp & Weave, Volume 18 Issue 1, 2019

"She Was Only Scared"
Touchstones: Journal of Literature & Art, Volume 32 Issue 1, 2019

Acknowledgements

This book would not have been possible without the love and support from my family and the MFA program at the University of Baltimore. I would like to specifically thank my thesis professors, Betsy Boyd and Jane Delury, my "Thesis Pieces" editorial group Kylie Catena and Kayla Tellington, and my peers Ashley Krumrine and Jack Livingston. Without my friends within the MFA program, I would not have been able to produce this beautiful book. Thank you to my thesis design professor at the University of Baltimore, Tony Fyre, for his guidance and to my professor at Utah Valley University, Deb Thornton, for their teachings on typesetting.

Under Water was years in the making, but the process started during the first course of my MFA program, "Creativity: The Way of Seeing" taught by Betsy Boyd. In this class, I was directed to run one of my poems into N+7. N+7 regenerates writing by taking a random noun, counting seven down in the dictionary, and replacing the word. After doing this activity, my line "blossoming fairytales" changed to "bluebottle fairytales."

I had never seen "bluebottle" written as one word before, which was intriguing. Curious about what the word meant, I quickly fell down a rabbit hole of research. And when I discovered a bluebottle jellyfish cannot survive by itself, I began working on what later became this book. I can truly say *Under Water* would not be what it is today without my MFA program.

For anyone considering an MFA in creative writing, the one piece of advice I have for you is to go for it! You never know what knowledge you don't have until you learn it. My MFA program not only gave me a valuable education but also inspiration, motivation, and support to achieve my dreams.

Beautiful Books. Unique Stories.

Elizabeth Publications is the publishing imprint of
Diana Elizabeth Clarke's books.

Professional book services are available. Services include book
design, editing, ghostwriting, and writing tutoring.

elizabethpublications.com

This book was typeset within Adobe InDesign with typefaces Minion Pro (paragraph), Bookmania (title), and Savoye LET (sub-title).

All artworks are original and done by the author. The cover art is an acrylic painting on blue cardstock. Interior art includes pencil sketches and digital art created within Adobe Fresco, Illustrator, and Photoshop.